The Mountain

To,
  Ahana &
       Meghna
With love & Best
           wishes
Mashi dida, Dadu,
       30.12.14.

The Mountain of the Moon

Bibhutibhushan Bandyopadhyay

Translated from the Bengali by

Jayanta Sengupta

Rupa & Co

Published 2011 by
Rupa Publications India Pvt. Ltd.
7/16, Ansari Road, Daryaganj,
New Delhi 110 002

Sales Centres:

Allahabad Bengaluru Chennai
Hyderabad Jaipur Kathmandu
Kolkata Mumbai

Printed in India by
Nutech Photolithographers
B-240, Okhla Industrial Area, Phase-I,
New Delhi 110 020

This is for Khuku

Bibhutibhushan Bandyopadhyay
Barrackpore, Jessore
1 Ashwin 1344

Author's Note

The Mountain of the Moon is not a translation from an English novel, nor is it inspired by any similar story from another land. The story and the characters in it are all products of my imagination.

However, in order to present realistic descriptions of various geographical areas of Africa and its various natural scenes, I have taken recourse to the books written by many famous travellers in Africa, like Sir H.H. Johnston and Rosita Forbes.

In this connection, I would like to mention that the Richtersveldt mountains referred to in this story is a very well-known range of mountains in Central Africa, and the many stories and myths surrounding the Dingonek (Rhodesian Monster) and the Bunyip are still prevalent in the forest areas of Zululand.

I am indebted to the late Mohinimohan Chattopadhyay for the translation of the poem by St Franco Sor.

Bibhutibhushan Bandyopadhyay
Barrackpore, Jessore
Ashwin, 1344

Translator's Note

I read *Chander Pahar* for the first time when I was five years old. A young lady friend of mine, who is unfortunately no more, gave it to me on my birthday. I remembered that the edition I read was illustrated with some lovely stark black and white drawings by Satyajit Ray.

Many years later, in my mid fifties, I found that old book – slightly battered by the intervening ages – and read it once again. Some pages had gone AWOL, the cover was attempting to play truant at every available opportunity, and the book was only held together with a string, cellotape, and faith. Re-reading it after nearly fifty years, the memories of my childhood, the birthday party, the little girl who gave me the book, the reading of the book sitting with my grandmother in her house in Asansol – all of these came flooding back. And, more to the point, the tale was just as gripping as I had found it at the age of five.

The power of the story had not faded one iota with time. Shankar's boredom at the prospect of life as a clerk in a jute mill was just as palpable, and his hankering after adventure in the Dark Continent just as urgent as I had remembered.

That was the moment when I decided to attempt a translation of *Chander Pahar*. Yes, I knew that other translations existed. But once the bug bites, you got to do what you got to do, without thinking about such mundane matters like whether the work will ever see the light of day.

Bibhutibhushan Bandyopadhyay was a voracious reader, and if there are similarities between *Chander Pahar* and H. Rider Haggard's *King Solomon's Mines* (to name just one great adventure story), that does not diminish the Bengali masterpiece at all. Rider Haggard's book is the first English adventure novel set in Africa, and has sometimes been called the 'genesis of the Lost World literary genre'. It is more than likely that Shri Bandyopadhyay would have read the English novel. In the author's note, Shri Bandyopadhyay had acknowledged the debt he owed to travellers who had written about Africa. Also, there are very significant differences between Shankar and Allen Quatermain, the English adventurer and traveller based in Durban (South Africa) who is the hero of *King Solomon's Mines*. The lower middle-class Bengali boy from a village some distance away from Kolkata was as different as could be imagined from Quatermain. Hence, the fact that Shankar could be the hero of the adventures described in *Chander Pahar* could, arguably, make the Bengali book a greater work of fantasy than Rider Haggard's book. After all, the British had contributed a significant number of adventurers, explorers, and travellers to the world; the Bengalis had contributed not a single one that I can recall.

Shri Bandyopadhyay had also obviously read J. H. Patterson's *The Man-Eaters of Tsavo and Other East African Adventures* for describing the incidents involving the man-eating lions in *Chander Pahar*.

The finicky reader will find many little quibbles in the original – for example, there are references to *baagh*, which would typically mean tigers, and of course there are no tigers in Africa. But does it reduce our pleasure in reading the book? Not at all!

Similarly, a quick Google search will show that the Richtersveldt is an arid area, and is today regarded as the only arid biodiversity hotspot on Earth; a far cry from the impenetrable forested land that it is described as in *Chander Pahar*. Incidentally, I have used the spelling 'Richtersveldt' instead of 'Richtersveld' throughout – based on the same principle: does it matter? No, not a bit!

What about the *Bunyip*, which claimed the lives of Jim Carter and perhaps Diego Alvarez as well?

According to *http://www.britannica.com*, 'Bunyip' is not an African legend at all! 'In Australian aboriginal folklore, [a Bunyip is] a legendary monster said to inhabit the reedy swamps and lagoons of the interior of Australia. The amphibious animal was variously described as having a round head, an elongated neck, and a body resembling that of an ox, hippopotamus, or manatee; some accounts gave it a human figure. The Bunyip purportedly made booming or roaring noises and was given to devouring human prey, especially women and children. The origin of the belief probably lies in the rare appearance of fugitive seals far upstream; the monster's alleged cry may be that of the bittern marsh.'

Not that Africa is devoid of legendary monsters. Here are some notes on the Dingonek:

- *http://www.unexplained-mysteries.com* has explained Dingonek in some detail. 'Hailing from the Congolese jungles (primarily in the nation formerly known as Zaire), the Dingonek is yet another in a long line of West African cryptids – such as the CHIPEKWE, the JAGO-NINI, and the EMELA-NTOUKA . . .
- Said to dwell in the rivers and lakes of western Africa, the Dingonek has been described as being approximately twelve feet in length, with a squarish head, a long horn, saber-like

canines, and a tail complete with a bony, dart-like appendage, which (much like the Indian MANTICORE) is reputed to be able to secrete a deadly poison. This creature is also said to be covered head-to-toe in a scaly, mottled epidermis, which has been likened to the prehistoric-looking Asian anteater known as the pangolin.

- The Dingonek has been accused of being an extremely territorial animal, and has been known to kill both crocodiles and hippopotami, which have trespassed into its domain. This violent disposition has also found its fair share of human victims, as many unwary fishermen – who have had the distinct misfortune of straying into this beast's domain – would surely attest.'

- In *http://www.strangeark.com/bfr/historical/dingonek.html*, Edgar Beecher Bronson describes 'that infernal horror of a reptilian "bounder" that comes up the Maggori River out of the lake the Lumbwa have christened Dingonek . . . holy saints, but he was a sight – fourteen or fifteen feet long, head big as that of a lioness but shaped and marked like a leopard, two long white fangs sticking down straight out of his upper jaw, back broad as a hippo, scaled like an armadillo, but coloured and marked like a leopard, and a broad fin tail, with slow, lazy swishes of which he was easily holding himself level in the swift current, headed up stream.' (1910, 'In Closed Territory', Chicago: A. C. McClurg.)

- In *http://www.cryptoarchives.com/1900/1930*, Vernon Breisford describes a number of Rhodesian monsters, sufficient to satisfy the most fastidious reader.

- In *http://afraf.oxfordjournals.org/cgi/pdf_extract/XXXIX/ CLIV/61*, P.A.T. Simey also describes a few such monsters.

Again, would it disturb the reader to know that Shri Bandyopadhyay transplanted the Bunyip from Australia to Africa without so much as a by-your-leave? 'Not at all' would be my guess.

While preparing these notes, there are a few things which I thought required some explanation to today's reader. I am mentioning these at the risk of sounding pedantic – and if you are not bothered to read these notes, who would blame you? Jump straight to the story and enjoy yourself!

But for those few who might want to read the notes, here they are for what they are worth:

- The author mentions that Shankar has passed his FA examination. This refers to an old educational milestone called the 'First Arts' examination, which is now defunct. There is also a reference to an 'Entrance Class'. Since this has nothing to do with the story, the reader would do well to ignore this piece of information.

- In Part II, Chapter I, the engineer in charge of the construction project addresses Shankar as 'Roy'. At the end of the book, J G Fitzgerald's letter to Shankar addresses him as 'Mr Choudhuri'. Shankar has been mentioned as such in the original, hence I have not attempted to make this consistent. Perhaps Shankar's surname was 'Roy Choudhuri', and contemporary usage allowed the use of either half of the surname or the whole of it.

- The author's note and dedication carries the date 1 Ashwin 1344. It converts to 16 September 1937 using the results provided by the website – *http://www.pallab.com/services/bangladateconverter.aspx*

- In the author's note, there is a reference to a poem by St Franco. This is also quoted in a Bengali translation in Part

12 of this translation. I must confess that I have not been able to track down the original poem, nor have I been able to find out if the poet in question was St Franco or St Franco Sor! I console myself with the thought that this is not intended to be a work of scholarship, so I could be excused from not doing proper and extensive research. The English version that I have written in Part 12 is my translation from the Bengali text. Hence, any resemblance it may have to the original Spanish (or Portuguese) prayer is purely coincidental.

In the final section (Part 14), the author quotes from a Chinese proverb. This time I can say with some pride that I have done some research on this, and I am indebted to Ms Jennifer Ng of Hong Kong for tracking this down for me. According to her, the source is the '*Book of the Northern Qi Dynasty: the biography of Yuan Jingan*' (《北齊書 元景安傳》 in Chinese), and this was probably written or compiled in the year 550 in the modern era. The original in Chinese is '寧為玉碎，不作瓦存', and the exact translation is – 'it is much better to be a shattered piece of jade lying on the floor rather than to be a tile on the corner of the roof.' According to Ms Ng, 'The meaning of this proverb is never stoop to compromise . . . or someone should rather lose their precious life (break a crystal/jade into pieces) than change their mind to accept something valueless (tile).' This seems to be a perfect expression of Shankar's view of life.

While reading *Chander Pahar*, it struck me that Shankar's peregrinations had caused him to cover an enormous amount of ground all over sub-Saharan Africa. Starting from the railway construction camp, some 350 miles to the west of Mombasa, he travelled to a small station near Kisumu, then by steamer to Mwanza, and then on to Tabora and Ujiji, and so on. While trying to plot his journey on a map, I was impressed by the thousands of miles he had traversed in his adventure – from Mombasa to Salisbury. The adjoining map makes no pretence of being accurate – it just indicates the rough route of his travels.

If you, like me, wish to locate some of the place names in the maps of modern Africa, I should tell you that many of the names have changed, and I couldn't locate some of the places on the maps I consulted. Albertville is now called Kalemie; Rhodesia is Zimbabwe and Salisbury is Harare. I couldn't find Knudsberg (or is it Noodsberg?) or any town by a similar name on any map of the Uganda Railway; neither could I find Sankini – this could be Kisangani, that's in a completely different direction from what is written in the book.

I also failed in my search for authenticity of all the African place names mentioned in the book. For example, in Part 10, the author mentions that the name of the volcano in the ancient Zulu language was Oldonyo Lengai, which means 'The Bed of the Fire God'. In the maps and histories I consulted, there is a mountain called 'Ol Doinyo Lengai' which means 'Mountain of God' in the Masai language.

However, such little discrepancies, and my failure to locate the places on the modern map of Africa should not in any way take away from the pleasure of reading the book. In most cases, the places mentioned in the book do exist even today. Mombasa does exist, so does Kisumu, Victoria Nyanza, and also Ol Doinyo Lengai, the Kalahari Desert, the Chimanimani Mountain, the Kruger Mountain exists as Kruger National Park, and many other places that Shree Bandyopadhyay describes in *Chander Pahar*.

And in the final analysis, the pedantic issue of whether the places are authentic or not is completely immaterial for us to enjoy the pleasures of the book. After all, we have all enjoyed the pleasures of *The Lord of the Rings*, or the Harry Potter books, or Arthur Conan Doyle's *The Lost World* and indeed Rider Haggard's *King Solomon's Mines* without caring one whit about their geographical or historical authenticity. They are what used to be called 'rattling good yarns', and that's why they live on in our minds.

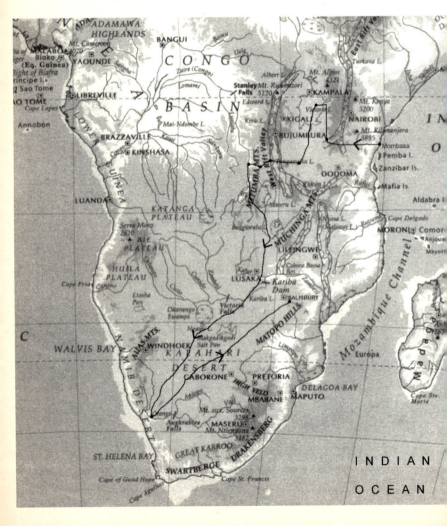

To me, perhaps to most of you reading this book, Africa is still an unknown continent. Africa means the Sahara Desert, the Pyramids, lions, elephants, giraffes, and the South African cricket team, and that's about it for most of us. As a teenager, *Chander Pahar* inspired me to read more about Africa and find out more about its enchanting history. As an adult, it inspired me to read about the exploits of David Livingstone, Henry Stanley, Sir Richard Burton, John Speke, and other explorers who opened up the Dark Continent in all her beauty and enchantment.

I hope you enjoy reading this translation as much as I have enjoyed writing it. And I really hope it encourages you to read the original if you can. Perhaps it will encourage you to explore the other masterworks of Bibhutibhushan – that would be the greatest joy of all.

12 December 2010

Jayanta Sengupta
Mumbai, India

Part 1

Chapter 1

$\mathscr{S}$HANKAR ROY HAD JUST RETURNED FROM CALCUTTA TO his home, a small village far away from the cities of Bengal. His FA examinations were over, and he now whiled away his days with his friends from the village in the mornings; a long siesta after lunch, and fishing in the evenings in small ponds, or in the river near the village. That was all the work he had to worry about.

After most of the summer had passed like this, one day his mother called him. 'There's something I need to tell you, Shankar,' she began. 'Your father has not been keeping well for some time. I don't know whether you'll be able to study any further. How will we pay for your studies? Whom can we ask for money? You should start looking around for a job.'

His mother's words got Shankar thinking. He too had noticed his father's illness over the past few months and how it was becoming increasingly difficult for him to meet his expenses in Calcutta. Now it was going to be virtually impossible.

But back in 1909, five years before the World War in Europe, the market for jobs was not so bad. With a little effort, people could find themselves decent jobs. There was a gentleman from the village who had got a job in a jute mill in Shyamnagar, or perhaps it was in Naihati. Shankar's mother went to his house and spoke to his wife about finding her son a job in the mill. The next day, the gentleman came to Shankar's home to say that he would do his utmost to help him.

After all, Shankar was not an average run-of-the-mill village boy. Very active since his childhood, he had always excelled in sports in his school days. Recently, he had won a medal for the first prize in high jump during the district sports. He was the best centre forward in the area, and was the undisputed swimming champion as well. He had also excelled in riding horses, climbing trees, and boxing. While staying in Calcutta, he had practised boxing regularly at the YMCA. Had he put half of this dedication into his studies, he would have easily got a first class. As it was, his devotion to sports had relegated him to a second class.

There was another subject that fascinated him. Reading books on geography, poring over maps of various countries and locations was a passion of his. He was an expert in solving geographical problems using mathematics. He was familiar with almost all the constellations that he could see in the sky. Ursa Major, Cassiopeia, Scorpio, Orion – he knew the names of all and could tell which constellation rose above the horizon at what time and in which month. This kind of knowledge was very useful in earlier times but during these days, very few people knew or even cared to learn it.

This time when he came home, he had brought with him a whole bundle of books on geography, astronomy, travel and related subjects. He would sit alone in a corner of the garden and read them, and look afar into the horizon – thinking god knows what.

But now, time was rude to Shankar. First came his father's illness, then little touches of poverty in the home, and now his mother's request to work in the jute mill. What should he do? He couldn't bear to see the signs of suffering in his father's eyes nor could he ignore the pleas on his mother's face. So, whether he liked it or not, he would have to take up a job, any job, wherever he got it, even in a jute mill.

But that would destroy the dreams that he had so carefully nurtured – to become a famous centre forward, to become the high-jump champion in the district and the state. But no, fate seemed to have decreed that he would be a clerk in a jute mill. Soon, he would wake up early in the morning, pack his paan in a small nickel-plated tiffin-box, put his kerchief in his pocket, and run as soon as he heard the first whistle from the factory. He would come home sharp at twelve noon, have lunch and go back to the factory. When the factory blew the whistle at six in the evening, he would return home.

Shankar's youthful mind rebelled at the thought. His body and soul fought against the very idea. Was a thoroughbred race horse finally destined to become a nag drawing carriages in the streets of the city?

It was a little before sunset. Sitting on the river bank, Shankar thought about the crossroads where his life had taken him. He had always wanted to fly away to far-off lands, to various parts of the globe, doing deeds that called for courage, bravery, adversity, and adventure. Like Livingstone, like Stanley, like Harry Johnston, like Marco Polo, like Robinson Crusoe. He had prepared himself mentally and physically for a life such as theirs.

He had never even considered the thought that what was possible for boys and men from other lands was virtually impossible for those from Bengal. They had been created to become clerks, schoolmasters, doctors or lawyers. To tread on the road untrodden, to reach the horizon unreachable – that was not the fate of Bengali boys and men.

In the dim light of the diya, he opened the big geography book by Westmark. He reached for his favourite section of the book – the description of the ascent of a huge mountain called 'The Mountain of the Moon', by the German explorer Anton Hauptmann. He was really fascinated with this section and had read it hundreds of times, and, every time he read it, he had told himself that one day, one day, he would go and conquer the mountain of the moon, just like Herr Hauptmann.

Stuff of dreams, he knew they were! As if the mountain from the moon would ever come down on earth! The real mountain would always be afar, always beyond reach.

That night, he had a dream.

He was surrounded by a dense bamboo jungle. A herd of wild elephants was feasting, and the sound of breaking bamboo shoots was loud in his ears. He and one other companion were climbing the huge mountain. The scenery around them was exactly like that of the mountain of the moon that Hauptmann had described. The same dense bamboo jungle, the same huge trees covered with liana creepers, the same thick carpet of rotten leaves. Through the gaps in the trees, he could sometimes see, far in the distance, the bare sides of the mountain, and sometimes its peak clad in permanent snow, bathed white in the moonlight. Often, this was hidden from view by the jungle. Through the tree cover, he could see a few stars in the clear sky. Suddenly, he heard the loud trumpeting of the elephant herd. The whole jungle shook at the sound. This sounded so real that Shankar woke up with a start. He sat up with a jerk in his bed. It was dawn, and the early rays of the sun had come into his room through the rods in the window

What a wonderful, beautiful dream! *Maybe this would come true. People said that dreams you had at dawn came true. Maybe there was truth in this belief.*

Chapter 2

THE VILLAGE HAD AN OLD, BROKEN-DOWN TEMPLE — VERY old and very broken down indeed. Legend had it that Madan Roy, the son-in-law of one of the Barobhuniyas, had built this temple many, many years ago. The family and their relations had died out. The temple was now in ruins; peepul and banyan trees had grown in what remained of the walls and in the corners of the cornices of the ceiling. But the altar was still quite intact, as was the *bedi* on which the God's *pratima* had been installed. There was no *pratima* there any more, but the villagers still religiously performed puja on Saturdays and Tuesdays, the village women came every day and put *sindoor* and *chandan* on the *bedi*. It was said that the God was very powerful and listened to everybody's wishes. If you prayed for something with your heart and soul, the God would surely grant you your wishes.

Shankar went to the temple after a bath. He tied a stone in a string, and then tied the string to one of the roots of the banyan tree. He also made a prayer to the God.

In the afternoon, he sat on the grass in front of the temple, and stayed there thinking for a long time. The small square was overgrown on all sides by bushes, and was quite lonely. On one side was a large house in ruins, where somebody had been murdered when Shankar was an infant. The owners of the house had moved elsewhere since then, and the place had now acquired a reputation of being haunted, and so was left alone by the villagers. Shankar really liked the quietude and the loneliness of the place, and came here quite often to get away with his thoughts.

The dream he had at dawn had left an indelible mark on his being. Sitting in the lonely little place, he relived the dream – the sound of wild elephants breaking down the bamboos, the sight of the snowy white peak of the mountain through the curtain of leaves and creepers in the trees growing in the cols of the mountain range, as if the snow-covered region defined the limits of some dreamland. Shankar had had many dreams in his life, but this dream was more real than reality; this dream had shaken his very consciousness like nothing else before.

But this dream would end up as a dream, he thought. He would have to take up the job in the jute mill – perhaps that's what was written in his fortunes, on his forehead, in his palms.

Chapter 3

$\mathcal{I}$N THE MORNING, SHANKAR WENT FOR A WALK ON THE BANKS of the river. When he came back home, the wife of Rameshwar Mukherjee from the neighbourhood came up to him with a piece of paper in her hand. She said, 'Baba Shankar, we have finally found out the whereabouts of our son-in-law after all these years. He recently wrote to his father in Bhadreshwar. Yesterday, Pintu came to visit us from there, and brought the address on this piece of paper. Please read it out to me.'

Shankar said, 'Thank God! After nearly two years you have some news of him! He gave everybody around quite a scare after he ran away from home. He had run away from home once earlier, hadn't he?' He opened the piece of paper and read out loud, 'Prasaddas Bandyopadhyay, Uganda Railway Head Office, Construction Department, Mombasa, East Africa.'

The paper dropped from his hands. East Africa! The man had gone really far, very far indeed. Shankar knew that the husband of his neighbour Nanibala didi was indeed a very curious man – vagabond, intensely curious, hyperactive, and totally stubborn. Shankar had met him once, in this village, when Shankar had just got into the entrance class. The man had struck him as being generous, quite well-educated, but flighty, which was why he could never stick to one job for long.

He had run away once and had fetched up in Burma or Cochin or some such faraway place. This last time, he had a major difference of opinion with his eldest brother and had run away once again. But this time, he had gone off as far as East Africa!

The wife of Rameshwar Mukherjee couldn't quite grasp where her son-in-law had gone. She had little idea of such distances. Shankar wrote down the address in his diary before giving her back the paper.

Within the week, Shankar wrote to Prasadbabu.

Did he remember Shankar? He was just a neighbour of the village into which Prasadbabu had married. Could Shankar get a job in the railways too? He would go wherever the company wanted to send him, he decided.

The weeks passed without Shankar getting any letter from Prasadbabu. Then, nearly six weeks later, after he had given up all hopes of a reply, an envelope came with his name on the cover. It read:

> Mombasa
> No 2, Port Street

Dear Shankar,

I have received your letter. I remember you very well indeed. You beat me in arm-wrestling and almost broke my wrist – how can I forget that!? You want to come here? Come over, Shankar! If young men like you don't leave the cocooned life in a small village and travel the world, who else will? The company is building a new railway and will need to hire a lot of people. Come over as soon as you can. I am taking the responsibility of getting you a job here.

> Yours sincerely,
> Prasaddas Bandyopadhyay

Shankar's father was really very happy on reading the letter. As a young man, he too had been adventurous and stubborn – the idea of his son becoming a clerk in a jute mill was not something he could accept easily; only the need for money in the family had forced him to agree with Shankar's mother.

About a month later, Shankar got a telegram from Bhadreshwar: Prasadbabu had recently come home, and would return to Mombasa in about three weeks. Shankar must meet him immediately on receipt of the telegram so they could go to East Africa together.

Part 2

Chapter 1

IT WAS NEARLY THE END OF MARCH, FOUR MONTHS SINCE Shankar had left his small village in Bengal.

The main railway line in East Africa ran from Mombasa to Kisumu, on the banks of the Victoria Nyanza. A new branch line was under construction, nearly three-hundred-and-fifty miles to the west of Mombasa, some seventy-two miles south-west of the Knudsberg station on the Uganda railway. Shankar was based here as the clerk and official storekeeper of the construction camp.

He lived in a small tent, in a village of tents set up in concentric circles in a large clear area, surrounded by a wide, open prairie, sprawled out as far as the eye could see, covered with long grass, punctuated by trees. Right next to the tent village was a large baobab tree, the famous tree of Africa, which Shankar had seen in pictures so many times. Seeing it for real was something special. Shankar could hardly take his eyes away from it.

In this new land, in these free and uninhabited grasslands and forests of Uganda, Shankar found bliss, and fulfilment of his long-cherished dream. This was what made his youth purposeful; this was what made his existence meaningful. Every evening, once he finished his work, he would set out from his tent, exploring all directions. On all the sides of the tent village, the savannah was covered with tall grass, in some places as tall as a man, in others even taller.

One day, the engineer in charge of the construction project called Shankar. 'Listen, Roy, don't go out for walks like this. Never leave without a rifle. First, you can lose your way in these grasslands. Many people have got lost wandering about in this place and died for lack of water. Second, Uganda is a land of lions. Because we make a lot of noise with our pickaxes, hammers and charges, the lions have moved away some distance, but they are not very far away, take it from me. You got to be very careful – these parts are most unsafe.'

One afternoon, the work was in full swing after the luncheon break when, suddenly, they heard the scream of a man. It came from an area of tall grass not very far away from the tent village. Everybody, including Shankar, ran towards that area to find out what had happened. They searched the whole area inch by inch, making their way through the tall grass, removing them strand by strand. But they found nothing, absolutely nothing.

Then what was the scream about?

The engineer joined the search party. He took a roll-call of all the coolies. One name was missing. His mates revealed that the man had gone into the long grass a little while ago, but no one had seen him return.

After a lot of search, the party found the pugmarks of a lion on a patch of sand some distance away from the tall grass. The engineer followed the pugmarks for a long distance, his rifle at the ready. Far away from the tent village, behind a huge rock, he found the bloodied and torn body of the coolie. His colleagues brought him back to his tent, where he died before dusk. But in spite of a lot of search, they couldn't find any sign of the lion – the hullabaloo among the workers had probably forced it to abandon its victim and leave.

The very next day, the workers cleared away the tall grass for many miles in all directions surrounding the tent village. For the next few days, they spoke of nothing except lions, and the mysterious lion that had killed their comrade. Over time, this incident faded away from their memories and no longer remained an important topic of conversation. A month later, it had been all but forgotten.

Chapter 2

*I*T WAS A VERY HOT DAY, THE KIND OF DAY WHEN THE AIR is still and the sun burns your skin like hot charcoal. But soon after sundown, it cooled down. The workers collected dry sticks, branches, twigs and grass, and made fires in front of their tents, and sat huddled around the flames, trading news and stories.

Shankar sat around one of these fires, reading a copy of the *Kenya Morning News*. It didn't matter that it was five days old – in this faraway place, this was the only contact one had with the outside world.

Shankar had formed a close friendship with Tirumal Appa, a young man from Madras. Tirumal knew English pretty well, and worked as a clerk. He was an energetic, enthusiastic young man, who had run away from home because the call of the wild was irresistible. Throughout the evening, Tirumal spoke about his home, his family, his mother, his father, his young sister. He was very fond of his sister, the person he missed the most in his family. This year, he was planning to go home at the end of September, and ask the engineer sahib for two months' leave. Surely sahib would grant his request, Tirumal hoped.

It was night and it had become colder. Some of the fires subsided, and the coolies threw more grass and branches into them to keep them alight. Many of them went off to their tents to sleep. The moon was in the first fortnight of its monthly cycle and rose slowly over the horizon. The play of light and shadow and the long silhouettes of the wild, lonely trees made the savannah a mysterious and fascinating place.

Shankar loved the silent, frozen beauty of these nights in this far-off land. He sat leaning against one of the upright supports of a tent, and looked at the huge, uninhabited grassland in front of the village, while many random thoughts chased each other in his mind. Beyond that old baobab tree, the grassland was spread out as far as Capetown, dotted with many mountains, many forests, many ancient cities like Zimbari, dating from prehistoric times, deserts like the infamous and deadly Kalahari, lands of gold mines, and lands of diamonds.

Once, an explorer seeking gold mines had stumbled and fallen. He carefully examined the stone upon which he had stumbled, and realised that there were streaks of gold in it and in the surrounding rocks. That place, since then, had become one of the largest gold mines in Africa. Shankar had read many stories like this about this land. That was what attracted him to this place – the mysterious continent – the Dark Continent – the continent of gold and diamond, the continent of unknown tribes and cultures, the land of sceneries that one would never see elsewhere, the land of animals that one would not find elsewhere. How little had been discovered of Africa! How much was still waiting to be explored!

His mind whirling with such thoughts, Shankar dozed off, not knowing when. Suddenly, he woke up hearing a sound. He sat up and looked around – the moon had climbed a long way towards the zenith. The clear, bright moon made everything white and visible like in broad daylight, the fires had mostly died down, the coolies were covered up and fast asleep around the fires. There was no sound from anywhere.

Shankar suddenly sat up straight. Tirumal Appa had been sitting right next to him before he'd fallen asleep – where had he gone now? Had he gone inside his tent to sleep? But he hadn't said good night to Shankar.

Shankar was about to get up and go inside his own tent to catch some sleep when the air reverberated with the terrifying roars of a lion. It came from not far away, just a few hundred yards to the west of the tents. The very earth seemed to shake and tremble with each roar of the lion. The coolies woke up instantly; the engineer came out of his tent with his rifle. This was the first time Shankar had heard the roar of a lion in the wild. In this huge, endless grassland, the roars of a lion in full moonlight in the dead of the night created a veritable maelstrom within Shankar. It was not fear; it was a complex melee of emotions which he could not describe in words.

An old Masai coolie in the tent said, 'The lion has killed a man. He wouldn't roar like this unless he has killed one.'

One of the men, who shared Tirumal's tent, suddenly ran out shouting that Tirumal was not in his bed, nor in the tent.

That scared everybody. Shankar searched every corner of the large tent where Tirumal used to sleep, but in vain. Tirumal was not there. The coolies had already lit up torches and searched the entire tent village for Tirumal. They repeatedly shouted out his name – all to no avail. They couldn't find Tirumal, nor did Tirumal answer their calls.

Tirumal's mates closely examined the place where he had slept. There were clear marks of something heavy having been dragged out of his sleeping place and out of the tent. Near the baobab tree, they found pieces of cloth from Tirumal's shirt.

Instantly, everybody realised what had happened.

Armed with his rifle, the engineer led the search party, followed by Shankar and the coolies. They searched all around the tent village through most of the night, and covered a large area in their search, but without success; they couldn't find Tirumal's body.

They heard the roar of the lion once more, but now it was from far away. The primal Goddess of the plains had claimed her sacrifice.

The old Masai said, 'The lion is taking away its kill. It will make our lives miserable now. No more will it be satisfied with any other meat; it will search and kill only humans. We have to be very, very careful from now on – a lion that has become a maneater is a very clever, shrewd and alert animal.'

When everybody returned to their tents, it was nearly three o'clock in the morning. The moon had lit up the whole of the plains as far as the eye could see. A nocturnal bird called from far away – a song of unearthly beauty, which, on any other night, would have sounded really sweet. The coolies prepared to go off to sleep once more. It had been a terrifying and tiring night for all. They put together all the grass, branches and twigs they could gather and built a giant fire, and sat huddled or lay down on the ground around the bonfire.

Shankar couldn't summon the courage to sit outside his tent. It seemed more than a little foolhardy to him. He lay down on his bed and stared at the grassland through the little window of his tent.

Tirumal's fate had brought him to Africa to satisfy a lion's hunger. Who knew why Shankar's fate had brought him to Africa?

Africa was beautiful, but her beauty was terrifying. The green plains and bushes reminded Shankar of his native Bengal; but while Bengal was peaceful, quiet and cosy, Africa was beautiful but deadly. Death dogged you at every step here. It could trap you any moment, particularly when you least expected it.

Africa had taken her first sacrifice – the young Tirumal. But that one sacrifice won't satisfy her; she wanted more.

Chapter 3

TIRUMAL'S DEATH SIGNALLED THE BEGINNING OF ENDLESS trouble for the residents of the camp. Maneating lions lose all fear of humans, and become very clever in searching out their preys and killing them. Living in the camp became very dangerous and well-nigh impossible. Even during the day, the workers stopped travelling more than a few hundred yards from the camp. Before dusk, they began to light big bonfires in the camp as well as throughout the surrounding fields and spend their evenings sitting around the campfires, cooking food, having dinner, exchanging hopes and fears, and chatting about the events of the day. The engineer began to take rounds of the tents at night and fire blank shots from his rifle, hoping to scare away any lion wandering nearby.

However, all this care and alertness proved futile. Two days after Tirumal's death, the maneater took away its second victim. The next day, a Somali coolie went to break rocks some three hundred yards from the camp – he never returned.

The same night, it was after ten o'clock when Shankar was returning from the engineer's tent. Everybody had finished his food and was back in his own tent, trying to sleep in spite of the fear of the maneater. Some of the bonfires had died down; the rest were burning low. From far away, Shankar could hear the hunting cry of foxes. It reminded him of his home in Bengal, his village, the trees in his garden, and the big hog-plum tree next to his house. He leaned on the front post of his tent and closed his eyes.

The sight before him was beautiful. Was he really in Africa, or had he been magically transported back to his beloved village? Was he standing in a camp, or was he in the little verandah of his home? If he opened his eyes, would he see the bonfires and the baobab trees, or the hog-plum tree with its branches spread out and leaves that gave such a pleasant shade in the hot summers?

Shankar slowly opened his eyes.

The huge plain was dark. The grass waved gently in the breeze. The baobab tree stood tall at the edge of the camp, like a monster out of the stories of demons and giants he had heard in his childhood. Suddenly, he thought he saw something. He looked carefully – something was moving on top of one of the tents. Something that shouldn't have been there at all.

The next moment, he stood frozen with fear. A huge lion was digging a hole through the straw covering the tent. Every now and then, it would lower its nose to the hole and sniff at something.

The tent was no more than fifteen yards away from Shankar. He realised that he was in great danger. The lion was busy digging the hole, intent on getting its next kill, and had not noticed Shankar. There was not a single soul outside the tents in the camp; nobody ventured out of the tents in the evenings for fear of the maneater. Shankar could not depend on anybody for help. And he was totally unarmed, without even a stick – not that a stick could keep a maneating lion at bay!

Shankar started walking backwards, step by step, one at a time, as fast as he could, towards the engineer's tent. One minute passed...then another...a third...he was getting closer. He kept his eyes fixed on the lion, avoiding even a blink. He had not realised until now that he had such control over his emotions, his body, his nerves. Never once did he feel the need to blink, the need to make a sound, or the urge to turn around and run as fast as he possibly could.

After what seemed like ages, he reached the engineer's tent. He lifted the flap and looked inside. The engineer was still at his table, engrossed in work. Before he could ask anything, Shankar put his finger on his lips and whispered, 'Sahib, lion!'

The engineer jumped up. 'Where?' He took his trusty Mannlicher .375 from the rack and gave another rifle to Shankar. They lifted the flap of the tent gently and silently stepped outside. They could see the top of the tent on which the lion had been trying to dig – but, there was no lion!

Shankar gasped, 'I just saw a lion on that tent! It was digging into the straw!'

The engineer said, 'It must have sensed something. Couldn't have gone far. Wake up everybody. Now!'

In a few moments, everybody was out of their tents, with whatever arms they could lay their hands on – sticks, clubs, picks, shovels, spades. They searched throughout the camp, in every tent, in every bush bordering the camp. They found the hole that the lion was digging and had almost succeeded in completing. They even found pugmarks of the beast. But of the animal itself, there was no sign. It had vanished completely, as if it never existed.

The workers re-lit the bonfires and built a few more. There was no question of further sleep that night – but nobody had the courage to stay outside their tents. Inside, at least, there was safety in numbers.

It was early in the morning. Shankar was in his tent, catching some blessed sleep when he was woken up by a big commotion, punctuated by shouts of 'Simba! Simba!' A rifle fired two rounds. He rushed out of his tent. A lion had attacked a mule in the stables, just next to the tent village. Thankfully, the mule was still alive; the lion had not been able to kill it and take away the body.

The next day at dusk, a young coolie was killed, not a hundred yards away from his tent. Four days later, another coolie was killed under the baobab tree.

Work became impossible. The workers were too scared to leave the camp. On the long railway line, they had to form small teams to work on various sections of the line. Nobody was ready to join such teams and move more than a hundred yards away from the camp. On the other hand, staying in the camp did not guarantee safety either – the incident of the lion in the camp was fresh in everybody's mind. Fear had cast its winged shadow on everybody's mind. No one knew when the maneater would strike. Each person thought that it was his turn next.

Only the Masais were unaffected. They did not fear anything or anybody, not even the devil himself. They did all the work on the line some two miles away from the camp, and the engineer visited them four or five times every day, with his rifle at the ready.

The engineer and his men tried everything they could think of, but it made little difference – the lion continued its depredations. The engineer and Shankar tried their best to hunt down the lion but all their attempts were doomed to failure.

A group of experienced coolies said that there were a number of lions: if you killed one, another would take its place. The engineer disagreed: this was the work of just one lion; maneating lions were loners.

Chapter 4

One day, the engineer asked Shankar to visit the Masai teams working in the vanguard of the railway line. Shankar agreed and asked him for his Mannlicher.

Riding a mule, Shankar went off to see the Masai teams. It was three in the afternoon of a burning hot day. He had reached a little swamp about a mile from the camp, and was about to prod his mule to move faster when he saw the animal freeze.

The mule refused to move forward. Something had scared it. Was it the large bush a little ahead on the path? Shankar got off the mule, and sensed rather than saw a very slight movement in the bush. Or was it a sudden waft of breeze?

Suddenly, Shankar was electrified by a thought – what if it was the lion, lying in wait for him in that bush? He had read that lions followed their target for miles, stalking them through grass and bushes, without giving the victim the slightest clue of the presence of the killer. Suppose the lion had decided that Shankar was going to be its next meal, then?

Deciding that discretion is the better part of valour, Shankar turned the mule towards the camp – it would be foolish to proceed further. At that moment, there was a movement in the bush and, with an earth-shattering roar, a huge grey creature leaped upon the mule. Shankar, who was a few yards ahead, sprang round and fired two rounds at the lion. He couldn't tell if any of the bullets hit its target, but the lion turned around and vanished into the plain in an instant. The mule was badly injured and was thrashing about in pain. Shankar put him out of misery with a bullet and walked back to the camp, keeping a very close watch around him, taking utmost care that he was not caught unawares from the rear.

On hearing Shankar's account, the engineer said, 'The lion must have been hit. At that distance, it must have been. And if it has, it must be injured – badly.' Search parties went out looking for blood marks in the brush and on the ground. They found nothing – no marks of blood, no bits of skin or fur to indicate that a lion had been injured.

Chapter 5

$\mathcal{I}$T STARTED RAINING IN THE BEGINNING OF JUNE, MAKING things worse. As it was, living in fear of the depredations of the maneater was difficult. On top of that, the rains turned the fields into a swamp. The swarm of flies and other insects made the camp unfit to live in.

They decided to shift the camp.

Shankar did not go with the rest. He was transferred to a new place – he'd got a job as the stationmaster of a small station about thirty miles from Kisumu. Within a few days, he packed his belongings and moved to his new home.

Part 3

Chapter 1

$\mathcal{S}$HANKAR WAS VERY EXCITED ABOUT HIS NEW JOB AND HIS new charge when he reached the little station at about three in the afternoon. The stationmaster's room was tiny, the platform was made out of dried earth, which, along with the room and the surrounding area, was fenced with barbed wire. Behind the station was his living quarters – another tiny room, even smaller than the station room, just a bit larger than the proverbial pigeonhole.

The train that had brought him here steamed off towards Kisumu, and left Shankar completely alone. He felt like a tiny drop in a huge ocean. He had never imagined that there could be such a lonely spot on earth!

He was the only employee, in fact the only human being, at the station. He was the stationmaster, the pointsman, the coolie – all rolled into one. There was a reason for this. The railway company was concerned about the need for such tiny stations, and since these stations did not make enough money, the company was not willing to spend too much on them. The first train was in the morning, the next one had just left in the afternoon, and that was that – there were no more trains the whole day.

Shankar had a lot of free time on his hands now. His immediate task was to take over charge from his predecessor, a nice Gujarati gentleman, who spoke English pretty well. He explained the tasks of a stationmaster to Shankar over a cup of tea. He was very happy to meet Shankar – it looked like it had been a very long time since he found somebody to speak with.

They walked around the platform and the station area. Shankar asked, 'Why the barbed wire fence?' The Gujarati gentleman answered, 'Oh! Nothing much to worry about, really. This is such a lonely spot, the company thought that the fence would provide some security.'

Shankar's instinct told him that something was wrong here. Something unsaid, something that his companion did not want to talk about, something that Shankar must know. However, he did not wish to push his new friend that night.

The Gujarati made a simple dinner of chapatis and vegetables, and invited Shankar to join him in this spartan meal. Suddenly, in the middle of dinner, the Gujarati clapped a hand to his forehead and exclaimed, 'Oh God! I completely forgot!'

'What's the matter?'

'There's no drinking water at all! I should have got some off the train, but it totally slipped my mind!'

'What do we do? Is there no drinking water available here?'

'None at all! There is a well nearby, but the water there is bitter and acidic. You can clean utensils with it, but you can't drink it. You need to take drinking water from the train.'

Quite a place, Shankar thought. Not a soul, no drinking water. Why the railway company made a station here was a mystery.

The Gujarati left the next morning. Shankar was left completely alone. He did his work, there wasn't much of it, cooked and had his meals, and stood on the platform when the trains came by. In the afternoon, he did some reading, or stretched out on his large work table and slept. Around dusk, he stepped out on the platform and strolled about.

The station was in the middle of a huge savannah, covered with long grass, dotted with yucca and acacia trees. In the distance, a long range of hills fenced the savannah on all sides. A very beautiful place and a really wonderful scene, Shankar thought.

Chapter 2

*T*HE GUJARATI HAD TOLD HIM NEVER TO GO OUT WANDERING into those fields alone. 'Why?' Shankar had asked, but hadn't got a satisfactory reply.

He got his answer that very night.

It was still quite early. Shankar had just finished dinner and sat down at his work table to write his diary. Thinking it would take some time, he'd decided to sleep in the station room that night. The glass door from the platform to the room was closed but not latched.

A slight noise made Shankar look up from his diary – a huge lion was standing on the platform, looking in through the glass. A slight push, and the door could open and the lion could come in.

Shankar froze. He was totally unarmed. There was only the wooden ruler on the table. Not very useful in defending himself against a lion.

The lion stared at Shankar, the table and the kerosene lamp on the table, with almost a look of wry humour. It must have been no more than a couple of minutes, but to Shankar it seemed like he and the lion had been looking at each other for ages. Then, slowly, the lion turned and sauntered away, down the platform, with an air of indifference. Shankar quickly got up and latched the door.

'Now I know why the station and its surroundings were fenced with barbed wire,' Shankar thought. But he was only partially right. The rest of the answer came a few days later, and from a different direction altogether.

When the train came next morning, Shankar narrated the whole incident to the guard. The guard was a friendly soul and listened patiently. 'It's the same story all around here. Twelve miles from here, there's another small station, just like this one, and the situation there is equally bad. There's another thing about your station...Oh, we have to leave now.'

He was about to say more, but stopped himself, and jumped into the train. While the train was steaming away, he shouted out to Shankar, 'Be very careful, always be on your guard.'

Shankar was worried. The Gujarati man, the guard, both were on the verge of saying something important to him, but had stopped short. What was it that they were trying to hide? Was there any other problem with the station besides the lion? Was it cursed in some way?

Anyway, worrying won't help matters, he decided. From that night onwards, Shankar began lighting a large fire on the platform outside the station room door. Just after dusk, he entered the room, locked the door from inside and read and wrote his diary till late into the night.

From time to time, he stared out. The grasslands were completely invisible in the darkness, except for the moonlight. The wind blowing through the yucca tree on the platform made a muffled crying sound. Out in the savannah, every now and then he could hear the crying of foxes and jackals. Sometimes, deep in the night, from afar came the roaring of a lion.

A very strange life, indeed! But this was exactly the life he had wanted, he had craved for. This huge, uninhabited savannah, this mysterious night, this pitch-dark sky filled with numerous stars which he, the amateur astronomer, could not recognise, these days and nights tinged with ever-present danger. To him, this was life, not the safe, peaceful, predictable existence of a clerk, running from home to work and back with a lunch box in hand.

One day, he sent the afternoon train off on its way and went towards the little kitchen of his living quarters. Something next to the door jamb looked a little out of place. Shankar took a closer look, and leaped back onto the platform. A large yellow cobra stood next to the door looking at him, fangs at the ready, its forked tongue flicking in and out, ready to strike. If Shankar had noticed it a second later...no, he didn't even want to think about that! Now he had to figure out how to kill it.

The snake didn't wait for Shankar to make up his mind. In a quick slick move, it crept up the door post and hid inside the straw cover of the hut. The same hut which Shankar would now have to enter to cook his food. This wasn't a lion which he could hope to keep at bay with a fire and a latched door.

After some hesitation, Shankar went into the kitchen and somehow cooked his dinner, ate and cleaned the utensils. He then escaped to the comparative safety of the stationmaster's room before it became quite dark. But now it didn't seem to be much of a refuge. The snake could get in from any little hole or crack. What would Shankar do then?

The morning train brought Shankar some relief. The guard and a new coolie dropped off his rations. Railway employees in such faraway postings got their rations of rice and potatoes twice a week from Mombasa, the price of these was deducted from their monthly pay.

The coolie was an Indian, in fact another Gujarati. After delivering the things, he looked at Shankar strangely, and very quickly jumped back into the train, as if he was afraid that Shankar would ask him something.

What were they all trying to hide? Shankar had not missed the strange behaviour of the coolie. What mystery was hidden in this little, harmless-looking station? Why was nobody willing to tell him?

A couple of days later, after sending off the afternoon train, Shankar was about to step into his little room when he shied back – he had almost stepped on a yellow cobra. It could have been his old acquaintance, or another one of the same species. Either way, he had no wish to get to know the snake any better.

Shankar thoroughly examined the platform, the station room, his quarters, and the surrounding area. There were holes and cracks and mice droppings everywhere. So, the snake must have come to feed on the mice.

Chapter 3

*L*ATE ONE NIGHT, SHANKAR WAS FAST ASLEEP ON THE TABLE in the station room. It was dark; the fire had burnt out. The grassland was black. As black as only Africa could be on a moonless night. Suddenly, he woke up.

Some hidden sense, other than his normal five, had woken him up with a very strong and urgent message: *'Danger! Danger! You are in danger of your life!'* Shankar sat up shivering, unable to see anything in the complete darkness of the room. He felt around him – where was his torch? A faint sound came from within the room. Suddenly, his hands found the torch. He switched it on, and sat like a wooden puppet at what he saw.

A few feet from his table, between him and the wall, was something which would strike anybody with fear even in broad daylight. Frozen momentarily in the light of the torch, ready to strike, was the most fearsome, the most dreaded snake in the whole of Africa – the black mamba. It had its head raised four feet from the floor. Shankar had read a lot about the black mamba – it was known to strike a fleeing man on his neck. To escape from it would be no less than a rebirth. Would he be given the chance of a rebirth this time?

Shankar had been blessed with an exceptional quality since childhood – in times of danger, he never lost his nerve. He could keep his head cool even when all others around him panicked.

He realised that if his hand shook for even a moment, if the torch swerved from the mamba for even a fraction of a second, the snake would strike. He knew that his life depended on keeping his hand absolutely steady and his torch focused on the eyes of the black mamba.

Shankar sat on the table with his hand rock steady, the light from the torch fixed on the eyes of the mamba. What anger and hatred did those two burning beads contain? What strength and speed did that slim, lithe body possess?

Shankar forgot about everything else in the world. The table, the walls, the door, the room, the platform, the station, the railway line from Mombasa to Kisumu, Africa, India, his home, his village, his parents – nothing existed anymore. The whole of existence was centred on those two beads of light. Outside them, there was absolute nothingness, total blackness. Like death. Like the world after the final destruction.

The only truth in the world was the black mamba – its raised head and fangs that could inject 1500 milligrams of deadly poison into him.

Shankar's hands were frozen. His fingers, his whole arm were losing sensation. How long could he hold onto the torch? Were the two beads of light really the eyes of the mamba? Were they not a pair of fireflies? Were they not stars he could see through the window? Was the torchlight as bright as before? Was it not becoming dim? Were those beads of light not coming closer?

Shankar pulled himself together. He had to remain alert; he couldn't afford to be bewitched by those eyes. In the middle of this savannah, there was not a soul he could call for help. Nobody would hear his shouts. His life depended entirely on his self-control.

But his arm was becoming weak. How long could he keep it straight and pointed at the snake? He had to take a chance, he had to put his arm down a little, switch the torch to his other hand. *Perhaps the snake won't strike him while he was doing so?*

The station clock struck three.

Certainly Shankar had a lifeline beyond three o'clock that night. As soon as the clock struck, his hand shook, and those bright yellow beads vanished.

But where did the black mamba go? Why didn't it strike him?

Immediately, Shankar understood that the snake too had been under the spell just like him. This was his one chance. Quicker than lightning, Shankar leaped off the table, unlatched the door, ran onto the platform, closed the door and latched it from outside.

He spent the rest of the night walking about the platform. When the morning train came in, he told his story to his friend, the guard. The guard said, 'Let's take a look around the rooms.' Nowhere in the station could they find any sign of the black mamba.

The guard continued, 'Let me tell you something. You had a miraculous escape last night. I didn't tell you this earlier for you would have been scared. The Gujarati station master, who used to be here before you, ran away because of the snake. Two other station masters before him had died of snake bite. Nobody lives anywhere close to a place known to have black mambas. I am telling you all this as a friend, don't tell others that you have heard all this from me. Perhaps you should apply for a transfer.'

Shankar said, 'That's a good idea. But it will take time to get a reply, let alone a sanction to my application. In the meantime, you can do me a favour. I am completely unarmed here. Could you get me a rifle or a revolver on your next trip? And I need some carbolic acid. Could you get me a bottle on your return?'

He got a coolie to stay back at the station for a while. Working through the day, they closed all the holes and cracks they could find in the station area. After examining closely, they found one large crack in the western wall of the station room, through which the mamba might have come. The crack was made by rats – obviously, the snakes had come to the station area to hunt for them. The coolie and Shankar filled this crack as best as they could.

The guard on the down train gave them a large bottle of carbolic acid, which they spread all over the platform, the station room and Shankar's quarters. Before he left, the coolie took out a huge stick from the train and left it with Shankar. A couple of days later, the railway company sent a rifle to Shankar, which gave him a feeling of safety in this godforsaken place.

Part 4

Chapter 1

WATER WAS A HUGE PROBLEM AT THE STATION. THE WATER ration left by the passing trains was just about sufficient for cooking and drinking, but shaving and bathing were out of question. The well too had run dry in the burning heat of the savannah.

One day, a coolie, on a passing train, told him that there was a large watering hole some three miles away. The water there was supposed to be pretty good for drinking, and what's more, he had heard from hunters that it also had fish.

The idea of having a bath and, of course, the possibility of augmenting his paltry meal with fish were very tempting for Shankar. One morning, after the train had departed, he and a Somali coolie went looking for the watering hole. Shankar had got himself a fishing rod and tackle from Mombasa a few weeks ago, and this was the first time that he had the chance to use it.

The watering place was quite large, surrounded by tall grass and yucca trees. Nearby was a small hillock. Shankar had his first bath in weeks, and then sat for a couple of hours fishing. He caught half-a-dozen small fish that reminded him of the ones he would catch in the ponds of his village back home.

He couldn't wait for long, he had to get back to the station by four o'clock when the afternoon train was to pass through.

After this, he started going to the place quite often, on some days with a coolie from the train or a rare visitor from the wilderness, but most often alone. Now, he could also have regular baths.

The already scorching summer got worse. This was the African summer he had read about – you couldn't go out in the sun after nine in the morning, after eleven o'clock it seemed that the whole plain, the grass, the trees, indeed the sky itself, were on fire. It was not much of a relief to be told by travellers that the summers of Central and Southern Africa were even worse.

On one such day, Shankar's life changed – forever. It began like any other day. After seeing off the morning train, Shankar went fishing. It was already three o'clock in the afternoon and he still had about a mile to cover. He was hurrying back to the station to meet the afternoon train when he heard a croak, like somebody in great pain trying to speak. Shankar stopped. The sound came again. Clearly, someone in distress was trying to draw his attention. Shankar searched carefully – there, under the little shadow of a yucca tree, someone was sitting, leaning against the tree trunk.

Shankar hurried to the man. He looked like a European. His clothes, that once must have been a good pair of trousers and a coat, were now rags – stitched and patched over many times. With a long red beard, big eyes, a large frame and a strong face, he must have once been a force to reckon with, someone you wouldn't take lightly. But he had, obviously, suffered from starvation, extreme exertion and possibly some disease. What else would have brought him to this wild savannah, where he could meet another human being only by chance?

He was at the end of his tether. His dirty sunhat had fallen on the ground. Next to him was a large khaki bag, held together with many stitches and patches, like his clothes.

Shankar asked him, 'Where are you coming from?'

The man held his cupped hand in front of his mouth, and whispered, 'Water! Some water!'

Shankar said, 'There's no water here. If you can come with me to the station, I can give you. Can you manage?'

Somehow the man made it to the station – at first leaning on Shankar and, later, by almost being dragged by him. By the time they reached, the afternoon train had long gone. Shankar made a bed for him in the station room, got him food and water, and saw to it that he was comfortable. The food and water infused some strength into the stranger, but Shankar noticed that the man had fever. Lack of food, physical suffering, and illness had taken their toll on him. He would take a long time to recover, Shankar thought.

Chapter 2

*B*Y EVENING, THE MAN RECOVERED ENOUGH TO TELL Shankar his name, Diego Alvarez, and that he had come from Portugal many years ago. The sun, the wind and the stars of Africa had turned his skin the colour of copper, like his hair.

However, as the hours passed, the fever seemed to increase. Shankar did not know what to do. There were no medicines at the station, no doctors anywhere close by. The morning train didn't go to Mombasa but further into the wilderness. There was only the afternoon train into which he could put the patient under the care of the guard. But the patient had to last till then!

Shankar sat up with Alvarez that night. His frame had broken down from the travels and the hardships he had suffered. And now, there was only Shankar to look after him and, hopefully, restore his health.

The moon rose from behind the hills to the north-east of the station. The trees and the grass shone in the moonlight. Shankar was standing on the platform, enjoying the breeze which gave some welcome relief after the heat of the day, and looking at the dangerous beauty of the savannah when suddenly the silence was broken by the roar of a lion. Alvarez woke up with a start, and his hands started searching blindly for a rifle. Shankar said, 'Don't worry, go back to sleep. The lion is quite far away, and we are safe behind closed doors.'

The lion continued roaring. It was no more than six hundred yards away from the station. But Shankar had got used to the calls of lions and other wild beasts by now. The beauty of the night, moonlight and shadow playing hide-and-seek in the tall grass, the yucca trees, the purple and black hills in the distance – all these mesmerised him; lions were now just part of the beauty of the plains.

He took a walk round the station and came back into the room. The clock had just struck two when Shankar noticed that the patient had sat up in his bed. He said, 'Could you give me some water?'

He spoke English well, Shankar noticed. He brought some water in a tin.

The fever seemed to have gone down a little. The man said, 'You thought I was afraid? Of the lion? I, Diego Alvarez, afraid of a lion? Young man, you obviously don't know anything about me.' The man leaned back on his pillow with a slight smile laced with pain, pride and sorrow. Shankar had an instinctive feeling that this was no ordinary man. He looked him over in the light of the candle.

He looked at his hands and noticed the strong, blunt fingers, creased, veined, with muscles like wires. He noticed the hard, jutting chin under the beard. The character of the man was becoming more noticeable now that the fever was passing.

He told Shankar, 'Come closer, I want to talk to you. You have helped me a lot. If you had not done so, I would have died in the wilderness. If I had a son, he wouldn't have looked after me any better. So, I want to tell you something now. I think my days are numbered. My heart tells me that I won't live for much longer. Before I go, I want to help you. You look like you are from Asia. Are you an Indian? How much are you paid for this job? If you have come so far away leaving your home for such a low pay, then you have courage. You can stand hardship and suffering. Now, I am going to tell you something. Listen to me very carefully. But you have to make a promise – whatever I tell you today, you have to keep it a secret as long as I am alive. Promise?'

'I promise,' said Shankar.

For the rest of the night, Shankar heard a strange and wonderful tale – the kind he had thought existed only in storybooks.

Part 5

The Story of Diego Alvarez

Chapter 1

'*H*OW OLD DID YOU SAY YOU ARE, YOUNG MAN? TWENTY-two? You were an infant cradled in your mother's arms, exactly twenty-two years ago, in 1888 or '89, the year I am talking about. I was prospecting for gold, north of the Cape colony, looking for a gold mine in the mountains, forests and deserts of Southern Africa. I was young then, as young as you are now, and for me dangers just did not exist.

'I left Bulawayo one day, with all my food, weapons, everything that I needed, all alone, with two donkeys to carry the load. I crossed the Zambezi River and went on. The land was new to me, the paths unknown. It was a flat savannah, dotted with tall grass, a few hills and, from time to time, the villages of the local tribes. After a few days, villages became more and more scarce and I reached a land which, perhaps, no European before me had ever reached.

'Every time I crossed a stream or came across a hill, I searched for signs of gold. Since my childhood days, I had read about how people became rich finding gold in Southern Africa. Such stories fascinated me. These were the stories that had brought me to Africa. For two years I travelled all over the continent, suffered many hardships, was tormented by diseases – all to no avail. Once, I thought I had found what I had been looking for. But I lost that trail as well.

'Early one morning, I went out hunting deer. Before noon, I had come back to my tent, cooked and eaten my meal, and set the meat out to dry. You can't travel in the wild after that. The heat was killing, the temperature was more than a hundred-and-fifteen degrees Fahrenheit. In mid-summer, it reached as high as hundred-and-thirty. When I woke up late in the afternoon, I started cleaning my gun. I noticed that the sight of my gun was not there. It must have dropped off somewhere and I hadn't noticed. I searched for it in my tent and the fireplace, but couldn't find it. I had to get a new sight, for without it you can't aim a gun. I went to a pile of rocks nearby, looking for a small stone which I could use as a sight. I found a number of small white stones strewn about, from which I chose one that I rubbed and polished till it could fit into the sight holder. I tried my rifle and it worked fine.

'Late afternoon, I struck camp and went northwards. I didn't make a note of the location, the pile of rocks, or any landmark nearby. Little did I know that this laxity on my part would come back to haunt me just a few weeks later.

Chapter 2

'ABOUT A FORTNIGHT LATER, I MET ANOTHER EXPLORER looking for gold, an Englishman accompanied by two Matabele coolies. His name was Jim Carter, he was older than me and, like me, he was a vagabond and a globe-trotter. We were happy to meet each other and got along well.

'One day, while examining my rifle, he was curious about my newly made gun sight. When I told him how I had lost the original and made a new one from a piece of rock, he got very excited. "You have no idea what this is. This is pure silver, from a strain of high quality. There must be a silver mine close to where you found this. In my rough estimate, you should be able to extract about nine thousand ounces of silver from one tonne of rock. Let's go back to your earlier camp, right now! We shall soon become rich!"

'Carter and I backtracked our path trying to find my old camp. For four months we searched. We went through much hardship, much suffering, got lost in the grasslands, found ourselves at the edge of the desert, got lost in the mountains, reached the threshold of death's door many times but never could find my old camp. In the African veldt, everything in all directions looks the same; there are no natural landmarks to help you. After many fruitless months, we decided to give up and go towards the Guai River. Jim stayed with me. He was with me till his death.

'I still remember his painful death.

'Suffering from thirst is possibly the worst suffering of all, or so it seemed to us travellers. So we decided that once we found a stream or river, we would travel only on its banks. We hunted in the forests or the veldt and, from time to time, if we found a village, we bought sweet potatoes, fowl, eggs and other foodstuff.

'Travelling like this, we crossed the Orange River and camped near a village about fifty miles upstream. That afternoon, the headman's little daughter fell very ill. A small girl of about five, she was rolling naked on the ground, crying that she had a very bad stomach pain. The whole village was in turmoil. She must have been possessed by an evil spirit, who would release her only on her death, they thought.

'Talking to the headman and other villagers, I gathered that she had gone to the edge of the forest and that's where the evil spirit had caught her. It was apparent to me that she had eaten too many wild fruits or berries, which was the reason for her stomach ache. I asked her whether she had eaten anything in the forest. She said that she had eaten some unripe fruits and particularly the seeds of these fruits that had tasted very good.

'A single dose of homeopathic medicine from my chest cured her. The evil spirit fled rapidly. And we became the toast of the village. We stayed there as guests of the headman for about two weeks. We hunted elands and other antelopes, and invited the villagers to share the meat with us.

'When we were ready to leave the village, the headman said, "White men love white stones! Very pretty white stones. You want those? Wait, I will show you."

'After a little while, he came back with a white stone the size of a large fig. Jim and I were astonished – it was a diamond! A real diamond. A rough, unpolished diamond from a mine or from the earth leading up to a diamond mine.

'The headman said, "Take this with you. Can you see those mountains in the distance? Hazy and smoky? You can reach those in a single moon. We have heard they are home to many such white stones. We have never been there and don't want to either. It is a very bad place. An evil spirit called Bunyip lives there. Many moons ago, some very courageous warriors from our village went to those mountains, against our wishes, and never came back. Another time, many, many moons ago, during my grandfather's time, a white man like you had gone there, he never returned either.

'Once we left the village, we sat on a large stone and tried to match the smoky mountains with those mentioned in the map. The mountains, hazy in the distance, were the Richtersveldt range – the wildest, the most unknown, the most dangerous, and the largest area in Southern Africa. Except for some intrepid travellers, or some explorer or geographer, nobody from the civilised world had ever set foot inside that area. Almost nothing about those huge forests and mountains was known, and the territory was virtually unmapped.

'Jim and I made up our minds immediately. We were going to be the first white men to set foot on the Richtersveldt Mountains. We were going to be the first to explore that area, the first to uncover the riches and wealth that so far had been hidden from the gaze of mankind. We had to go there.'

Chapter 3

'Some seventeen days after leaving the village, we entered the dense forest at the foothills of those mountains.

'I have already told you that these were in the most inaccessible part of Southern Africa. We didn't notice any villages or native settlements close to the forest. One look at it told us that an axe or a machete had never touched any tree or undergrowth here.

'We reached the edge of the forest a little before evening. We set up camp for the night. Jim collected sticks and twigs and we lit a fire. We had shot a couple of birds in the morning and I started to remove their feathers. I had planned to roast them for dinner.

'Jim wanted some coffee before the food, so I started preparing that. The roast would have to wait!

'I put on the kettle and started on the birds again when, suddenly, a lion's roar pierced the silence of the woods. It was very close to our campsite.

'Jim took up his rifle and went to investigate. I cautioned him not to go far since it was getting dark, and went back to the coffee and the birds.

'From somewhere in the forest a gun fired once and, after a few minutes, once more. Then silence. Minutes passed. I started to get a little anxious since Jim had not appeared as yet.

'I picked up my rifle and started going towards where the sound had come from. A little distance away, I saw Jim approaching, dragging something heavy. He saw me and shouted, "This lion has an excellent pelt. I didn't want to leave it in the forest. The hyenas would have eaten up the body – pelt and all. Let's take it to our camp."

'We dragged the huge beast inside.

'Soon it was night. We finished our meal and went to sleep.

'Late at night, we were woken up by the roar of another lion, not far from our camp. In the darkness, I couldn't judge the distance. I sat up and took my rifle. Jim said, "This one's the companion of the one I shot this evening," and then he turned over and went back to sleep.

'I went near the fire. It had died down, so I collected some more wood and set it afire again, and then I too went to sleep.

Chapter 4

'NEXT MORNING, WE STRUCK CAMP AND ENTERED THE forest. Sometime later we met some natives, out hunting deer. We asked them to join us as bearers and pathfinders, tempting them with tobacco.

'They refused point blank. "You don't know anything about these forests, that's why you are talking like this. We never go there. You should not either. You should go back. The range of mountains you see is not very high and once you cross this you will reach a flat land, covered with forest. After that comes another higher range of mountains. The forest in between is very dangerous. That's where the Bunyip lives. If you run into him, you'll never come back alive. Nobody goes there. No amount of tobacco will tempt us to risk our lives. If you value yours, you must leave these forests."

'We asked them, "What's a Bunyip?"

'They didn't know but were, very clearly, aware of the evil that it could do.

'Fear was not a part of our character, and Jim did not even know the meaning of this word. All this talk of fear and danger made him even more obstinate, almost obsessed, with going into the forest. He had to solve the mystery of the Bunyip, whether he found the diamonds or not.

'Little did I know then that death was calling him.'

The old man was tired after talking for so long. Shankar was captivated by now. He had never heard such a wonderful tale of adventure before. Looking beyond the torn clothes and the physical weakness of Diego Alvarez, he saw glimpses of the real man: the steely strength and fearlessness shining through the bright blue eyes from under the bushy eyebrows.

Shankar felt a surge of respect and affection for him. He had never met anybody like him before. This was a real man, he thought.

After a glass of water, Diego Alvarez started again with his tale.

Chapter 5

'THANK YOU. THAT WAS REFRESHING. NOW I MUST TELL you the rest of our story.

'We entered a dense forest. With huge trees, large ferns, many wonderful orchids and liana vines, it was virtually impenetrable. Even the undergrowth was almost totally impassable. The leaves and branches of the forest canopy were so intertwined, and the thorny bushes grew so tightly that perhaps even sunlight had hardly ever reached the ground. We couldn't see the sky.

'To make things even more difficult, we had to deal with hordes of baboons. Large families of babies, adults and older members of the tribe did not show any fear of us humans. Displaying their large teeth and screeching with rage, a few of the leaders were quite ready to attack us. Thankfully, our guns kept them off. Jim said that at least we wouldn't be short of food in the forest. The baboons would ensure that.

'We spent about a week in the forest. Jim was right. Everyday, we killed one baboon for food. We didn't suffer from thirst either – there were many streams coming down from the higher reaches of the range. However, we had to be careful about the water, and once we actually got into serious trouble by drinking from one such stream. One afternoon, we had just set up camp next to a small waterfall and were preparing to roast baboon ham for dinner when Jim drank some water from the stream. Pretty soon, he started vomiting and complaining about unbearable pain in his stomach. I suspected that the water he drank could be the source of the problem. I knew a little bit of chemistry, so I tested the water and discovered that it contained a lot of mineral arsenic, which must have dissolved in the stream water in the upper reaches of the range. I gave Jim a dose of homeopathic medicine from my travelling box and, by evening, he was a lot better.

'In the forest, we encountered only the baboons and a few poisonous snakes, but no other wild animals of any kind. But there were birds and butterflies aplenty. This tropical forest was a veritable paradise for ornithologists and lovers of Lepidoptera.

'The first representative of the Richtersveldt Mountains we came upon was a smaller range, lower in altitude, though from the foothills it looked deceptively like the main range. After crossing that, we entered a large forested valley where we set up our tents close to a tiny river that flowed through the valley floor. The river gave us hope. You can often find minerals and even precious metals on the banks of such rivers, which could lead you to the main sources of these materials.

'We used the traditional methods of prospecting – carefully and intensely combing the riverbed and the banks, and panning at many places, looking for a sign of "colour" or gold in the trail left after panning. Not a single grain of gold did we find. After twenty days of such backbreaking effort we started feeling quite dispirited. Would we fail once again after all this effort, energy and time, we wondered.

'While drinking coffee one evening, Jim said, "My instinct tells me that we will find gold here. Let's look around for a few more days." These "few days" became another twenty. We were sick and tired of our diet that seemed to consist exclusively of baboon meat. Even a patient person like Jim was feeling despondent. I said, "That's enough, Jim, let's turn back. The villagers have tricked us. There's nothing to be gained here." Jim was adamant. "This mountain range has many branches. I'm not going back without exploring all of them."

'One day, we were prospecting for gold on the bank of the river, when we discovered, almost hidden among a bunch of pebbles, a small stone that glinted yellow. Jim and I quickly dug it up. How happy and excited we were at our discovery! Jim said, "Diego, do you recognise this? Our efforts have finally been rewarded!"

'I was equally excited, but was still a little doubtful. "Yes, but this has been brought downstream by the river current. The source is not here but somewhere upstream."

'The little yellow stone was an unpolished diamond – the famous South African yellow diamond. That was good news, but not good enough for immediate celebration. All that it told us was that, somewhere in the vast mountains surrounding us, hidden somewhere in the unknown, dense, impenetrable forest, was the source of the diamond. The little stone was a tiny part of a layer of such diamonds, which had been swept away by the waters of the mountain stream. Many miles downstream, the river left the stone on its banks, to be discovered by us. Finding the source required almost inhuman toil, patience and courage.

'We would not have lacked for the toil, the patience or the courage. But the monster that guarded the doorways to the diamond mines, hidden deep within the mountain forest, caught us completely unawares.'

Chapter 6

'*O*NE EVENING, WE WERE RESTING IN A SMALL CLEARING IN the forest. In front was a palmyra tree, surrounded by dense bushes. Suddenly we noticed that the tree was being shaken, causing its branches and leaves to rustle loudly, just as they would in a storm. The tree was swaying to and fro.

'We were surprised. There was hardly any breeze, and the little there was, wasn't strong enough to make the tree sway. It looked as if some huge animal was shaking it.

'The ever-intrepid Jim entered the bushes near the tree to investigate. A little later I heard a scream, and ran in with my rifle. Jim was lying on the ground, bloodied, as if a strong creature had torn him open from his jaws to his chest with powerful claws – like you would cut open an old pillow to remove cotton from inside.

'All that Jim could say was, "It's the devil. The devil himself." He gestured me to flee, instantly.

'Those were the last words spoken by Jim Carter. A moment later, he was dead.

'I examined the tree. There were little pieces of skin and coarse hair stuck to its side, and some splinters broken off from the palmyra tree. It seemed to me that some extremely strong animal had rubbed itself against the tree, causing it to shake and sway. I could find no further trace of the animal.

'Rifle in hand, I dragged Jim's body to the clearing where we had our camp. I went back to the bushes to look for further traces of the creature. On the other side of the undergrowth, I found marks that the unknown animal had left on the earth – its feet had only three toes. I followed the tracks for a while. They disappeared into a cave some distance from our camp. On some dry sand just outside the mouth of the cave, Jim's killer had left its unmistakable mark – feet with just three toes.

'It was getting dark. In this uninhabited forested valley, surrounded by huge mountains, I was alone, trying to find an unknown but very powerful creature that had just killed my companion. On my right was a basalt wall rising about four thousand feet, covered with a dense forest of trees and tall bamboos, and right at the top I could see a tiny sliver of sunshine – or maybe I was wrong, maybe it was just the orange sky of sunset.

'It was not sensible to wait there or follow the tracks into the cave. I went back to the camp, lit a fire and kept watch over Jim's body by the fireside, sitting up the whole night with my rifle at the ready.

'The next morning, I buried him.

'Then I went in search of the unknown creature, trying to find the cave, which was obviously its lair. But try as I might, I could not find the cave again. On the mountainside, though there were many, I couldn't tell which cave I was looking for.

'It was not at all wise to stay on completely alone in the wild forests of the Richtersveldt Mountains. So I decided to return. After fifteen days, I found myself back in the little village from where we had started. They remembered and recognised me as the person who had cured the chief's daughter and looked after me well.

'I told them about Jim's death. Their faces turned white with terror when I told them about the animal that had three toes in its feet. "The Bunyip! Everybody's scared of him. That's why no living creature goes into that forest."

'From the village, I walked for five days to the banks of the Orange River, where I caught a launch operated by a Dutch company to bring me back to civilisation.

'I have never been able to get back to the Richtersveldt Mountains. Not that I have not tried. But fate intervened. The Boer Wars started and I enrolled myself, got injured and had to stay at the hospital in Pretoria for a long time before I was discharged. I got a job in an orange orchard where I stayed for a long time.

'But after five-odd years of a peaceful, orderly life, I couldn't stand it any more. So here I am, on the roads again. But, young man, I now realise that I am getting old. I think this will be my last journey. After this, I will find rest.

'Keep this map with you. In this I have marked, approximately, the Richtersveldt Mountains, and the river where we had found the diamond. If you have the courage, go there and search for it. It would be the making of you. After the Boer Wars, a few diamond mines were discovered near the Wai River in the same area. But nobody has yet explored the place where I had found the diamond. You must go there.'

Diego Alvarez finished his tale and lay back exhausted against the pillow.

Part 6

Chapter 1

$\mathcal{D}$IEGO ALVAREZ STAYED WITH SHANKAR FOR A FORTNIGHT and recovered slowly but surely under his care. But you can't tie down a ranger for long; for Alvarez, the road was his home. One fine day, Alvarez was ready to hit the road again.

By now Shankar had also reached a decision about what he was going to do. He asked Alvarez, 'Do you remember the story you had told me when you were ill? The diamond you found? The diamond mine you were looking for?'

After his recovery, the old man had not referred to any of the things he had told Shankar; he sat quietly most of the time, looking blankly into the veldt. Now he turned to Shankar. 'Do not think I have forgotten what I told you. I have thought about it myself. The question is – do you have the courage to chase a mirage?'

Shankar said, 'Let's put that to test. If you want, I can send a wire to the Maavo station, asking them to send somebody to replace me.'

Alvarez thought for a while, and then said, 'Send the wire. But before that, you must understand what awaits you. Those who search for gold or diamond don't always find it. I knew an eighty-year-old man who never found anything. Nothing at all. He often claimed he had reached the right trail, that this time, he was close to finding it. He never did. He spent his entire life prospecting in the deserts of Australia and the veldt of Africa.'

Ten days later, Shankar and Alvarez were on their way. They decided to go to Kisumu, where they would board a steamer which would take them south on Victoria Nyanza (Lake Victoria) on the way to Mwanza.

During their journey, Shankar was amazed to see thousands of giraffes, zebras, deer and antelopes on a huge plain – a sight he had never seen before. The giraffes were not at all scared of human beings. They stood and watched as the two men went by. Alvarez said that people needed a special licence to shoot a giraffe, and such licences were given sparingly, so giraffes were hunted very infrequently.

However, the herd of deer, two or three hundred strong, behaved differently. When the deer saw the two men, they immediately fled into the depths of the grassland.

At Kisumu, they boarded a British steamer on which they travelled on deck to save money. Negro women travelled with them with their babies tied to their backs and with their chicken and other belongings in tow. Masai coolies were going back home on leave, carrying with them their purchases from the Nairobi markets – glass beads, mirrors, cheap toys, knives, and various trinkets.

They disembarked at the port town of Mwanza and hit the road again. Some three hundred miles away was the town of Tabora, where they planned to rest for a few days, before proceeding to the town of Ujiji, an important port on Lake Tanganyika.

On the way, Alvarez told Shankar about the dangers of travelling on the Lake: the bite of the tsetse fly causes sleeping sickness, and an epidemic of this disease had killed a lot of people in Tanganyika. Also, the route between Mwanza and Tabora was so infested with lions that travelling in that region was very dangerous. This part of Africa could justly be called the kingdom of the lions.

Chapter 2

*T*EN MILES FROM THE TOWN OF MWANZA, THEY FOUND A small cottage built of grass and straw. A European hunter, who was staying there, greeted Alvarez like an old acquaintance. On meeting Shankar, he said to Alvarez, 'He is a Hindu boy! Where did you meet him? Is he your coolie?'

Alvarez replied, 'He's my son.'

The European was surprised. 'Your son?'

Alvarez told him the whole story of his travels, how he had fallen ill, how Shankar had rescued him and looked after him during his recovery. He did not speak a word about where he was going and why.

The European smiled and said, 'That's good. He looks like a good as well as a courageous man. Hindus from the East Indies are nice people. Once in Uganda, a Sikh showed me such hospitality that I can never forget it. I am in his debt forever. Well, you should spend the night here with me. This is a government dak bungalow. I am a traveller just like you. I reached here this afternoon after travelling the whole day.'

After a dinner of tinned tomato soup and sardines, the three took their camp chairs outside the bungalow and relaxed, listening to music from a small gramophone the European was carrying with him. Suddenly, a lion roared from pretty close by. It sounded as if it roared with its mouth close to the ground – the earth vibrated with each roar.

The European said, 'The lions of Tanganyika are very troublesome, very ferocious, and truly murderous beasts. Many of them are maneaters. Once they have killed and eaten a man, they won't settle for any other kind of food.'

Shankar's mind went back to his days with the Ugandan Railways. After all, he had first-hand accounts of trouble with lions!

Alvarez and Shankar left the next morning. The European had warned them about the dangers from tsetse flies and advised them to be very careful after sunrise: the flies woke up with the sun, and on no account should they be allowed to sit on their skin.

They travelled through small tunnels in the tall grass. Alvarez had told Shankar to be very careful about these grasslands. The lions took refuge in such tall grass, and the two men must never be separated.

While travelling with Alvarez, who was a crack shot, gave Shankar a little confidence, it did not amount to much. He knew from his experience in Uganda that when a maneating lion struck, it took its victim completely unawares. So much so that the victim would not have the time to even move the gun from his back to his shoulders.

A couple of hours before sundown, they decided to set up camp, in the middle of the huge veldt. Alvarez reasoned, 'There is no village close by, and it's not safe to travel in the dark in such a country.'

Under a large baobab tree, they hung two pieces of canvas – this was their tent, their home for the night. Shankar gathered some wood, lit a fire and made dinner. After the day's exertions, the two fell asleep quickly after their meal.

Late at night, Alvarez said, 'Shankar, wake up.'

Shankar scrambled up in his bed. Alvarez said, 'Some animal is circling our tent. Keep your rifle to fire at a moment's notice.'

Shankar could hear a large animal breathing, as it went around the tent. The remnants of the fire they had lit in the evening cast a hazy dark shadow of the baobab tree on their tent, making it look like a weird prehistoric monster.

Shankar tried to get down from his bed, but Alvarez gestured to him that he should stay where he was.

In the next moment, the animal hurtled itself against the wall of the tent, trying to force its way in. Alvarez fired twice. Shankar lifted his gun to shoot at the animal but, before he could press the trigger, Alvarez's gun fired once more. Then silence.

They lit a torch and very carefully stepped outside. Pushing against one side of the tent lay a huge lion. It was not dead yet, but very badly injured. Two more bullets made sure it was dead.

Alvarez looked up at the stars in the sky and said, 'There's a long way to go before dawn. Let the lion lie there. And let's get back to sleep.'

A little later, Shankar heard Alvarez snoring loudly. But Shankar couldn't sleep at all and stayed awake.

Half-an-hour later, it appeared to him that all the lions in Tanganyika were determined to outdo the snores of Alvarez. Each snore was being answered and bettered by the roars of a lion. Shankar had heard lions roaring many times before, but this was different – and it was from within twenty paces of their tent.

Alvarez woke up. 'Ugh! This is really intolerable. They won't let us sleep tonight. This one must be the companion of the one we killed. Be careful. This one's going to be quite a nuisance.'

It was a very difficult night for Shankar. The fire had nearly burnt out, so it was almost completely black outside the tent. Only the thin layer of canvas tent protected them from the dangers outside, which included the lion that had lost its companion and was vowing revenge. Sometimes the roars came close to the tent, sometimes they moved away, sometimes they circled round the tent.

A little before dawn, the roaring stopped and the lion moved away. A short while later, the two travellers lifted the canvas tent and set out again on their journey.

Part 7

Chapter 1

About two weeks later, Shankar and Diego took a steamer from the small port of Ujiji and crossed Lake Tanganyika to another little town called Albertville, where they bought many of the essentials for their journey. The Belgian authorities ran a small railway from here to Kabalo. Their plan was to take a launch from Kabalo to Sankini down the River Congo – a journey of three days – and leave the river and the well-trodden roads from Sankini. Turning southwards from there, they would enter the unknown land of jungles and deserts.

Kabalo was a dirty little town, overrun by an unruly mob of racist Belgians and Portuguese, with no morals and ethics.

Shankar had just stepped out of the station when a strange Portuguese man accosted him. 'Hello! Where are you going? I can see that you're new here, so you don't know me. My name is Albuquerque.'

Shankar noticed that Diego was still inside the station building.

Albuquerque was tall, nearly seven feet, strong, muscular, as ugly as Mother Nature could make him, and looked every inch a hard, unscrupulous man.

Shankar said, 'I am glad to meet you.'

Albuquerque said, 'A black man, most likely from the East Indies. Come, let's play poker.'

Shankar was already more than a little irritated by the behaviour of this stranger, so his response was not very polite, 'I have no intention of playing poker with you.' He had understood that the invitation was not to pass the time in a pleasant, innocent manner but was merely a ploy to rob him of his belongings. Although he had never played the game before, he had heard stories of how expert poker players in Nairobi had ruined many men by enticing them to play for high stakes.

Albuquerque was enraged by Shankar's refusal. His face turned red; his eyes were inflamed. With his face alarmingly close to Shankar's, he said, 'What? What did you say, you dirty little nigger? You seem to be quite a brat, not as well-behaved as most East Indians I've met. Let me tell you for your own good – Albuquerque and his revolver have killed useless nigger guttersnipes like you by the dozen. Let me tell you one more thing – I have this rule for all new people coming to Kabalo: either they play poker with me or fight with me and my gun. Now, what do you want to do?'

Shankar was in a bind. A gun battle with this rogue meant certain death. Albuquerque seemed a ruthless killer and, probably, a crack shot, while he was a meek Bengali boy, and a harmless railway clerk until a few weeks ago. But if he chose to play poker, he would be ruined for sure, thought Shankar.

Albuquerque drew his gun from the leather holster round his waist, pushed it against Shankar's stomach and shouted, 'Fight or poker?'

Shankar lost his head. As it was, he was already feeling insulted by the racial taunts of the Portuguese. He decided that he wasn't going to give in like a coward, but rather die fighting.

He was about to say 'I'll fight', when, from behind him, a loud voice broke in, 'Mind your head!'

Taken completely by surprise, both of them turned around. Alvarez was standing there with his Winchester repeater raised to his shoulders, aimed at the Portuguese. Shankar grasped the situation quickly, and moved away from Albuquerque's gun. Alvarez said, 'Fighting a gun battle with a mere boy? Ridiculous! Drop your gun by the count of three. One…two…' The gun hit the ground with a metallic clang.

Alvarez said, 'Showing off your prowess to a boy? Makes you feel proud of yourself, doesn't it? Why don't you choose someone your own size, eh?' Shankar had picked up the revolver by then and joined Alvarez.

Albuquerque looked very surprised. He had not realised that Shankar and Diego Alvarez were together. He smiled and stretched out his hand, 'I am sorry, mate. I lost, and please don't mind our earlier exchange. Give me my gun, my boy. Now look, there's nothing to worry about. And let's shake hands. You too, mate. Albuquerque is not one to nurse grudges. Come, let's go to my cabin and have a glass of beer.'

Alvarez knew people, particularly those of his own blood. He shouldered his rifle, and since the offer of beer sounded good, he took Shankar with him to the Portuguese's cabin. Since Shankar didn't drink beer, Albuquerque made coffee for him, and they spent a couple of hours talking and laughing as if they were old friends, far from the ones ready to fight to the death just a few minutes ago.

Shankar found the tall Portuguese man really fascinating. He had totally forgotten the enmity and insults of just a little while ago, and was merrily sitting with those who had made him swallow his pride. There are not many people like this in the world, he thought.

The next day, Shankar and Alvarez took the steamer from Kabalo to go south down the Congo River. Shankar felt so happy and excited looking at the scenery on both sides of the river.

He had never seen jungles like these before. The Africa he had known till now was a huge plain of tall grass, periodically interrupted by baobab, acacia and yucca trees. But the banks of the Congo River were altogether different– covered with very dense forests, different trees, large creepers, and a huge bouquet of wild flowers. Here, Mother Nature was mysterious, totally self-absorbed, enthralled by her own beauty.

Shankar might be thousands of miles away from home, but he still was a son of Bengal, a lover of beautiful things, a gentle poet at heart. Fascinated, from the first light of dawn till the last rays of the dying sun, Shankar looked at this new Africa and dreamed.

When everybody had gone to sleep, the forests came alive under the strange starry skies and the night was filled with the sounds of its residents. Shankar couldn't sleep – he absorbed the glorious nights in Central Africa through every single cell of his body. He saw the Great Bear shining, thousands of miles away. The same Great Bear he had seen in the skies of his village. He saw the sliver of the new moon, the same sliver he had seen hung in the skies back home. But he had left those familiar skies and travelled far, far away. How much farther he would have to go, only his fate could tell.

Chapter 2

*T*WO DAYS LATER, THEY REACHED SANKINI. FROM HERE THEY travelled on foot. The land was open country, like East Africa – huge, uninhabited plains covered with tall grass, forests and hills, some of bare rock with little green cover, some covered with euphorbia and other bushy growth. The abundant beauty filled his heart with delight and a sense of freedom – the colours of the sunset, the mystery of the moonlit nights, the shadow play of dusk. To Shankar, Africa was the true land of Faerie.

Alvarez told him to be very careful while travelling. Since the land looked the same in all directions, it was very easy to get lost.

Alvarez was probably prescient. On the very day he spoke the cautionary words, Shankar felt their truth. At sunset, they set up camp in the middle of the empty veldt and lit a fire to prepare food. Shankar went out to find water. He took Alvarez's rifle but only two cartridges. He wandered around for some time. The evening grew darker, slowly casting its shadow all over the plain. Shankar could have sworn that he had been away from the camp for no more than half an hour, when suddenly he felt disturbed, as if some danger was looming and he must return to the camp immediately. He looked around. The hills on the horizon, the tall grass in the plains, the trees – they looked the same in all directions. There were no landmarks to tell him which way to go to reach the camp.

He was lost. He remembered Alvarez's warning, but it was too late. He had not paid heed to the words of the veteran. He kept on walking. Sometimes he felt that the camp was straight ahead, sometimes on his right, sometimes on his left. Why couldn't he see the campfire? Where was the little hillock next to the campsite?

After a couple of hours, Shankar was really afraid. He had understood by then that he was hopelessly lost and was in the gravest danger, totally at the mercy of Nature. He would have to spend the night in this unknown veldt of Rhodesia, infested with lions, without the slightest knowledge of the nearest human settlement. And he would have to do it alone, without food or drink, without a blanket or fire to shield him from the cold. He didn't even have a matchbox with him.

The next evening, almost twenty-four hours after he had left camp, Alvarez rescued a disoriented and helpless Shankar from under a large euphorbia bush, some seven miles away from camp. Another few hours and he would have been beyond the reach of help.

Alvarez said, 'The road you'd taken would have carried you deeper and deeper into the grassland, away from the campsite. If I had not succeeded in finding you, by tomorrow afternoon you would have been dead. Many before you have died in the same manner. This is a very dangerous land; you must never leave camp like that in future. You're totally inexperienced, you don't know the techniques of survival in the plains, forests and deserts. You'll be dead in no time unless you learn, and learn fast.'

Shankar said, 'Diego, now you've saved my life twice over. I'll never forget this debt I owe you.'

Alvarez said, 'Young man, you forget that you saved my life much before all of this. If you hadn't come upon me that afternoon not too long ago, my bones would have turned white by now on the plains of Uganda.'

Chapter 3

About two months later, Alvarez and Shankar had crossed the big plains of Rhodesia and Angola and could see a line of high mountains far in the distance, hazy as clouds. Alvarez took out his map and, after a close look, said, 'That is our destination, the Richtersveldt Mountains, and we still have to travel about forty miles to reach there. The plains of Africa allow us to see things which are actually quite far away.'

Shankar saw a lot of baobab trees in this area. He loved these – from a distance they reminded him of the banyan and the peepul trees of his homeland. But up close they could not be mistaken for any other tree. They were huge but with little leaf cover, offering not much in the way of shade. With their crooked trunk and branches, and the strange marks like giant tumours or moles, the baobab looked more like the ugly, misshapen ogres from the Arabian Nights. The trees sprawled out over the huge plains of Rhodesia, as far as Shankar could see.

One evening, it was really cold. They had lit a large fire and, sitting in front of it, Alvarez said, 'You see this Rhodesian veldt, this is the land of diamond mines. There are diamonds all over this land. You must have heard of Kimberley mines, right? There are many other mines all over Rhodesia, and people have found many diamonds big and small scattered all over this land. They still do.'

Suddenly he whispered, 'Who are they?'

Shankar was facing Alvarez. He asked, 'Where?'

Alvarez's eyesight was as sharp as his shooting, and as accurate. A little while later, Shankar noticed some figures coming towards them out of the darkness. Alvarez whispered again, 'Shankar, get the gun, fast, and make sure they are loaded.'

When Shankar came out of the tent, Alvarez was smoking, sitting quietly as if without a care in the world, and the figures were much closer to the camp. Very soon, they entered the circle of light round the fire. They were tall and dark, well-built, empty-handed, wearing just a loincloth, with a band of lion's fur around their necks and plumes in their hair. In the firelight, they looked as if sculpted out of bronze.

Alvarez asked them in Zulu, 'Welcome! What can we do for you?'

After some conversation, which Shankar couldn't follow, the strangers sat down around the fire. Alvarez said, 'Shankar, please get some food for our guests.' In a very soft voice, he added, 'We are in great danger. Be very alert.'

Shankar opened the tins of food he'd got and placed them in front of the guests. Though they had already finished dinner, they had to join their guests for a second meal – either it was the local custom to eat with guests or Alvarez had something in mind.

While eating, Alvarez spoke with their guests in Zulu. After dinner, they left, accepting gifts of a cigarette each.

Alvarez was silent for a long while to make sure that the warriors were out of earshot. Then he spoke, 'They were Matabele warriors. They are very brave and very fierce, and have fought the British government and its armies many times. They aren't afraid even of the Devil. This place where we are camped belongs to one of their chieftains, and they are suspicious of our intentions. They think we've come to look for diamond mines. Here the only law is the word of their chief – the laws of any European authority just don't apply here. If they want, the warriors will take us to their village and burn us to death. Let's move camp from here.'

Shankar asked, 'Why did you ask me to get the guns?'

Alvarez laughed, 'If they were not convinced after our conversation, or if they seemed to have bad intentions towards us, I would have shot them while they were eating. Look, my loaded revolver was just behind my back. Even before they could reach for the tins of food, I'd have blown their heads off. My name is Diego Alvarez. I wasn't scared even of the Devil in the past, and am not scared now either, let alone a few Matabele warriors.'

Chapter 4

*A*FTER WALKING FOR ANOTHER WEEK, SHANKAR AND ALVAREZ entered the almost tropical forests in the foothills of a large mountain range. The forests were huge and showed no sign of human habitation. Shankar felt that if he ever got lost here, he'd remain so for the rest of his life. Alvarez again cautioned him, 'Shankar, you must be very careful and alert indeed while travelling in this forest. If you do not have the experience of going through a dense jungle, you can get completely lost. Many people have done so and died miserably. Remember the time you'd got lost in the plains? You could do the same in this forest. Every place here looks the same, and there are no landmarks to distinguish one from another. Unless you are a good and trained bushman, you'd be courting danger wandering about alone. You must always carry your gun with you – the Central African jungle is not a park for a picnic.'

Shankar had realised that himself. After a while, he asked, 'How far is the mine where you found the yellow diamond? From the map, as far as I can make out, this is the Richtersveldt Mountains range, isn't it?'

Alvarez smiled. 'You really have no idea what you are talking about. This is actually just the outermost range of the Richtersveldt. There are many such ranges that we have to cross. The whole area is so large that if you went eastwards for seventy miles, or westwards for a hundred to one-hundred-and-fifty miles, you'd still not be able to get out of these mountains or these forests. At their narrowest, these forests are still about forty miles wide. The whole Richtersveldt Mountains and forests area spreads over eight or nine thousand square miles. I had come here some seven or eight years ago. And you want me to remember exactly where I had come! Not an easy job, is it, young man?'

Shankar nodded and said, 'You do realise that we are running very short of food. Unless we start hunting from tomorrow, we'll have to survive on air!'

Alvarez replied, 'Don't worry about food. Look up – do you see all those baboons up in the trees? Even if we get nothing else, the hams of these will do us very well. Roasted ham and coffee will be our breakfast from now on. Now let's rest. We've travelled a lot today, and I am tired. Let's pitch our tent.'

They did so under a large tree, lit a fire and, after dinner, stared peacefully at the gathering gloom outside.

Alvarez lit his pipe and spoke, 'Do you know, Shankar, that there are so many animals, plants and birds here in this unknown Africa which modern European science is still ignorant about? Very few people from civilised countries have ever come here. The Okapi, for instance, was discovered only as recently as 1900. There is a species here of wild boar, nearly three times the size of the ones discovered earlier. Major Cowley, the famous explorer and big-game hunter, first got news of such a large wild boar only in 1888, in the Lualabu forests of Belgian Congo. After a lot of effort, he finally managed to hunt one such animal and gifted it to the American Museum of Natural History in New York. Have you heard of the Rhodesian monster?'

Shankar said, 'No, what's that?'

'Let me tell you about it. There's a huge marshland near the northern border of Rhodesia. The local Zulu tribesmen claim to have seen a very strange creature in the marshes from time to time. According to them, the creature has the head and tail of a crocodile, horns like a rhinoceros, the neck of a python, and a scaly body like that of a hippopotamus. This animal is very large and extremely ferocious. They've never seen it on land but only in the water. The descriptions by the native residents are typically highly exaggerated, so it is very difficult to believe them or take them seriously.

'However, in 1880, a prospector named James Martin spent a long time exploring that area in Rhodesia, looking for gold mines. Martin used to be the *aide-de-camp* to General Matthews, and was a very good geologist and zoologist. In his diary, he had mentioned about seeing this creature from a distance during his travels in this part of Rhodesia. He had also written that the animal reminded him very strongly of a dinosaur from prehistory, and that it was extremely large. But he couldn't be very specific in his descriptions because of the distance and he had caught a glimpse early one hazy morning, in the marshes at the edge of the Kavirondo Gulf. He and his party heard a whinnying cry like that of a horse, at which his Zulu servants and coolies started running away as fast as their legs could carry them. 'Run, bwana, run! Dingonek! Dingonek!' Dingonek is the Zulu name of the creature. It would be sighted not more than once or twice every two or three years, but had a reputation of being such a murderous beast that all the natives were extremely afraid of it. Martin had written that he had fired a couple of rounds from his .303 gun in the direction of the animal, but it was too far away for him to take proper aim. The creature had dived into the swamp on hearing the gunshots.'

Shankar asked, 'How do you know about all this? Was Martin's diary published?'

'Not that I know of. But I had read an article in the *Bulawayo Chronicle* that covered this incident. I had just reached Rhodesia at that time and, since I used to travel and prospect in the same area, I took a keen interest in the matter. I had kept the newspaper cutting with me for a long time but then lost it somewhere. The newspaper had given it the name "Rhodesian Monster".'

Shankar asked, 'Have you ever seen any strange animal?'

Silence all of a sudden. Evening had given way to night and, in the darkness, Shankar thought he saw a slight shudder run through Diego Alvarez's body. He thought he must be mistaken, for surely Alvarez was not afraid of anything. Or was he? Did the fearless, the unconquerable Diego Alvarez really fear something, after all?

He saw Alvarez take a quick, stealthy look around the campsite and at the forests and mountains surrounding them. He didn't say a word. To Shankar, it seemed that the question revived some old memory from his distant past. Unpleasant, painful and filled with horror. One that Alvarez would give anything to forget.

Alvarez was scared!

Shankar couldn't believe it, but yes, he was. Alvarez didn't want to show it. And seeing him afraid, Shankar started to feel scared himself. The dense forests and huge mountains surrounding them contained some deep mystery that they had hidden for ages. It was an invitation to every man of courage and bravery to come forward and unravel the mystery – but he would have to earn it the hard way, with his life as the stake.

The Richtersveldt Mountains were not like the Himalayas of India – the seat of Gods, the Emperor of Mountains. But, like the Masai, Zulu, Matabele and other cannibal tribes of Africa, were hungry and merciless. They would not allow anyone to escape their clutches.

Part 8

Chapter 1

A FEW DAYS LATER, THEY HAD REACHED DEEPER AND DEEPER into the forest. There were no paths, except what they had made for themselves, over hills and valleys, through the tall and rough tussock grass. Water was well-nigh impossible to get but, whenever they came across a mountain stream, Alvarez wouldn't let Shankar even touch it. Shankar found the clear, cool spring water irresistible. He longed to put his hands in it, collect it in his cupped hands and drink his fill. But Alvarez would make him drink only cold tea, which did nothing to slake his thirst. But still, Alvarez would not let him drink the water from the streams. Shankar felt that thirst was the most unbearable of all deprivations.

One day, they came to a place where the grass was particularly dense. The day was very foggy. Late in the morning, the fog suddenly lifted and Shankar found a steep side of the mountain standing in front of them, like a wall built to prevent them from climbing. It was so high that the top part was covered in a haze or by clouds, and he could not judge the height.

Alvarez said, 'This is the main range of the Richtersveldt.'

Shankar asked, 'Do we need to cross this range?'

Alvarez replied, 'Yes, because when Jim and I had come to the foot of these mountains, we had approached from the south. The river, on the banks of which we had found the yellow diamond, was flowing from east to west. This time, you and I are travelling from north to south and in order to reach that river, we have to cross this range – there's no other way.'

Shankar said, 'There's so much fog today, let's wait here for a while. Let the day progress for a couple of hours, and then we can lift camp and move again.'

So they rested a while longer. Even after lunch, the fog didn't lift. Shankar went into the tent to catch a nap. When he woke up, it was already late afternoon. Alvarez was studying the map, looking quite disturbed. He said, 'Shankar, we have problems ahead. Look at the mountains.'

Shankar took a closer look at the mountains and understood why Alvarez was looking so grim. The fog had lifted completely by then and all he could see were the various ranges of the Richtersveldt Mountains, like steps of a ladder going up higher and higher to touch the sky. The lower reaches of the mountains were covered with storm clouds, but the high peaks, lit by the colours of the setting sun, stood against the blue sky like golden shrines of the Gods.

Beautiful though they were, Shankar had to look at them with a more prosaic eye. The mountainside that he could see would be a very steep ascent indeed, with not a single easy slope in sight. Alvarez said, 'Shankar, we can't climb the mountains from this side, as you can see for yourself. We have to go westwards. We have to find some easier saddles from where we can cross the range. But it will take a lot of time, considering that the mountain range stretches some one hundred and fifty miles – that in itself is a task that would occupy us for more than a month!'

But luck was with them. After they had traversed westwards for some five or six days, they found a more suitable place from which they could attempt to cross the range. The slope was easier to tackle, and they decided to climb the mountain from here.

Early next morning, they started to climb. Shankar's watch showed the time as 6.30. After about two hours, he just could not climb at all! Even though the slope had looked comparatively easier than the other sides, it was difficult to climb and was really steep – they could cover only six thousand feet over a distance of four miles. In addition, the higher they climbed, the denser the forest became, and the darker it got. Though it was nearly late morning, inside the forest they could hardly see the sun; it was as if sunlight had never touched its floor.

There were no paths in the forest. Tree trunks stood like soldiers guarding the way up the mountain. The ground was moist, slippery and covered with moss – water must have been seeping out from somewhere. They had to be really careful: in case one slipped, he would go all the way down the mountainside – God knew where – and would certainly be badly injured by the sharp rocks, or even be dead.

Nobody spoke, nobody wanted to waste energy in speaking. The climb had made them both very tired, and they were breathing heavily. Shankar felt the strain a lot more than Alvarez. Having been born and brought up in the plains of Bengal, he had no training in climbing mountains.

Shankar was dying for Alvarez to speak the blessed words to stop and rest. But he had promised himself that even if he died, he wouldn't be the first to say 'Stop'. He felt he was a representative of India, of Bengal, and he would not let his motherland down by openly acknowledging his weakness to another man, not even to Diego Alvarez. He would not want him to think of men from the East Indies as unworthy.

The forest was magical, as if it was the kingdom of fairies. From time to time, they came upon small streams gurgling down the mountainside. From the branches, parrots and other birds flew overhead, creating a riot of colours. The tall grass was laden with white flowers; orchids hung from tree branches and tree trunks.

Suddenly Shankar noticed a tribe of what looked like pygmy monks sitting on the tree branches, with long whiskers and beards, and the solemn faces and bearings and quietude of true ascetics. He stopped in surprise. Alvarez said, 'These are the females of the Colobus monkey. The males don't grow beards and whiskers, only the females do and, as you can see, they are very stern in their demeanour!'

They couldn't feel the earth under their feet, only layers of rotten leaves and tree trunks and branches, probably as old as the earth itself. For centuries, leaves had been falling and rotting, moss and fungus had been growing on them, followed by more leaves, more moss, more fungus, as well as trunks and branches from dead trees. In many places, the layer of such dead leaves could well be more than sixty or seventy feet thick!

Alvarez taught Shankar how to walk in these forests carefully and place his feet with extreme caution. There were places where one careless step could suddenly lead to a man sinking through a hole hidden in the leaves, like stepping into the hidden mouth of a well. This could cause death by suffocation.

Shankar said, 'Unless we cut a path through the forest, we can't climb anymore.'

The elephant grass through which they were climbing was razor-sharp, like the double-edged blades of a Roman sword. Going through that was dangerous. One couldn't see ahead for more than a couple of feet. Also, one wouldn't know if a lion or an elephant or a poisonous snake was lying in wait, until it was too late.

Shankar noticed, from time to time, a sound like somebody playing a drum. He wondered aloud whether some local tribes were playing drums in the forest. Alvarez said, 'That's not the sound of a drum. There are no human settlements in this forest. Sometimes when a large baboon or ape thumps its chest, it makes a sound like that.'

Shankar said, 'But you had told me that there are no gorillas in this forest!'

Alvarez said, 'True, most likely there are no gorillas here. They have been found only in some parts of Belgian Congo, in the Rawenzi Alps, and the Virunga volcanic mountains. So we guess that they are not found anywhere else in Africa. But there are other apes that thump their chests like gorillas and make such sounds.'

Chapter 2

*T*HEY HAD CLIMBED FOUR-AND-A-HALF-THOUSAND FEET. They decided to pitch their camp for the night. Shankar couldn't sleep. The sounds of a tropical forest were so many, so mysterious and sometimes so fearful, that he had to stay awake – the laughter of a hyena, the harsh calls of a Colobus monkey, the sounds of an ape thumping its chest, the roars of a lion.

Nobody seemed to sleep at night in this huge natural zoological garden of nature. The whole forest woke up and almost went mad with sound at nights.

Some years ago, when Shankar was still in school, a large circus group had come to their village and set up camp on an open ground right next to the school hostel. Shankar remembered how the boarders could not sleep at night – the animals made so much noise that they kept everybody awake.

Shankar was really frightened when a herd of elephants went hurtling past their tent at night. He hurriedly woke up Alvarez. The latter said, 'Don't worry, go back to sleep. The fire is burning outside the tent – they won't bother us.'

They started climbing again in the morning, through miles and miles of wild bamboo forests, with an undergrowth of wild ginger. At one place they hid in the bushes, while a huge herd of elephants passed within a hundred yards, eating and crunching their way through the bamboo groves.

Up at five thousand feet the flowers were spectacular. The erythrina trees were in full bloom with their large, bright red blossoms. The flowers of the ipomoea creepers reminded Shankar of the flowers of the wild kalmia plants back home in his village, though the ipomoea ones were a darker shade of purple. The air was filled with the sweet smell of the white veronica flowers. The place also had flowers of wild coffee and begonia. Truly, a veritable paradise for nature lovers! This was a magical forest of flowers in the kingdom of clouds. Sometimes little heaps of clouds gathered in the topmost branches of the trees; sometimes they came down and wet the veronica bushes before going back up again.

It took Shankar and Alvarez another two days of back-breaking, lung-bursting climb to go up another two-and-a-half-thousand feet. At seven-and-a-half-thousand feet, the look of the forest changed completely. The tree trunks and branches were covered with moss – thick layers along with lichen hung from them. At places, they almost touched the ground, and swayed gently in the breeze. The sun couldn't penetrate the thick tree cover, so it was always twilight. And the whole forest was shrouded with an unearthly silence. Not a single bird chirped, not a single animal called. No rustling of leaves and, of course, no sounds of humans except those they made themselves. It was as if they had entered some dark unknown hell, where long-bearded ghosts were waiting for some unpleasant fate to befall them.

One afternoon, Alvarez stopped and ordered to pitch camp. They needed to rest for a while after the hard labour. Sitting on a rock outside their tent and drinking coffee, Shankar thought that the primeval forests must have been like this, when trees and plants were still unformed and unshaped by time and evolution, when the gigantic lizards of prehistory wandered through the dark forests. It was as if some time machine had taken them back magically to the beginning of life on earth.

By evening, complete, impenetrable darkness had covered the forest. The campfire cast a circle of light outside their tent. Beyond it, the world was black. The complete silence in this forest troubled Shankar. Never had he been to such a silent forest. What was the reason for this silence?

Alvarez examined his maps with an equally troubled look on his face. He said, 'You know, Shankar, something is bothering me. We have climbed more than eight thousand feet but have not yet found the shallow saddle where we can cross this range. How much higher would we have to climb? Suppose there is no such saddle in this part of the mountain?'

The same thought had struck Shankar too. Earlier in the day, he had looked through his field glasses to find some break in the mountain ahead of them but couldn't penetrate the fog and cloud cover to find any answer. He was just as worried as Alvarez. How much more would they have to climb? And suppose they didn't find any easy way of crossing the mountains here? Would they have to go all the way down, move in another direction at the base of the mountains, and try all over again? God forbid!

He asked, 'What about the maps? What do they say?'

The look on Alvarez's face indicated that he did not have much faith in the maps. He said, 'These maps are not that accurate. They are only indicative. Nobody has climbed these mountains or surveyed this area – so who would make an accurate map? Take this one. This was drawn by Sir Filippo de Filippi, the famous conqueror of the Ferdinando Po peak in the Portuguese West Africa. He was also part of the exploration team led by the great mountaineer Duke of Abruzzi. But he had never climbed the Richtersveldt Mountains.

The contours drawn on this map are not very faithful to the true layout of the land and are quite confusing as well.'

He stopped and Shankar exclaimed softly, 'What's that?'

There was a faint sound just outside the circle of light. This was immediately followed by the sound of someone coughing with a lot of pain, like someone suffering from phthisis. Once...twice...then the coughing stopped. But Shankar instinctively knew that it was not a human being who had made that sound.

He picked up his rifle and was about to leave the tent to investigate when Alvarez caught him by the wrist and forced him to sit down. Shankar was surprised. *What was that? Who made that sound?* Then he noticed that Alvarez's face had blanched – he looked very worried. Was it because of that sound? Had he heard it before?

Outside the tent, beyond the circle of light, they heard a light-footed large animal move away into the total darkness of the forest.

After a while, Alvarez broke the silence in the tent. 'Put some more wood in the fire. Make sure that both the rifles are fully loaded.' The look on his face prevented Shankar from asking any questions.

The night passed without much sleep.

Next morning, Shankar was the first to wake up. He went to collect some firewood for their morning coffee when he suddenly noticed something strange. On the wet earth next to a tiny stream, there was a footprint, at least eleven inches in length, and with just three toes pressed into the ground. On the other side of the stream, there were other such footprints. He followed these for some time – all the prints showed the three toes clearly.

Instantly, his mind went back to the tales Alvarez had told him in the little railway station in Uganda – the tale of how Jim Carter met his death, what the chief of the African village had told Carter and Alvarez, about finding the footprints of an unknown creature in the sand leading up to a cave. Footprints with three toes.

He also remembered the blanched, scared face of Alvarez the night before. He had looked so frightened just once before – the day they had made their first camp at the foot of these mountains.

Bunyip! The Bunyip of the story told by the African chief! This is the mysterious monster of the Richtersveldt mountains and forests. This is the creature who rules this kingdom through terror – terror that kept men, animals, and even birds from entering these forests above eight thousand feet.

Shankar now understood why he had heard no birdcalls or animal sounds the previous day. And Alvarez? Perhaps he had had previous acquaintance with that cough.

Alvarez woke up a little later. After some hot coffee and food, he looked once again the brave and courageous Alvarez, not scared of even the devil. Shankar did not tell him about the footprints he had discovered in the morning, fearing Alvarez would decide to go down and try elsewhere! If they did that, such a lot of effort would go waste.

Chapter 3

$\mathscr{I}$T STARTED RAINING. NO ORDINARY RAIN BUT A TORRENTIAL downpour. Water flowed down the mountainside like a thousand streams in spate. The rain made the going even more difficult and confusing. Even though they knew they were climbing up, every time they looked down the slope, the treetops looked so close that they would feel they had hardly gained any height even after such a lot of effort.

It rained the whole day. They waited till quite late in the morning for the rain to ease off, but there was no let up. Alvarez told Shankar to move camp. Shankar was disappointed – he had been looking forward to a lazy day inside the tent. What was the point in moving around on a day like this, getting drenched in the rain? What would they lose by waiting here just for one day?

But Alvarez was the leader and Shankar had to obey his instructions.

It rained the whole day. They climbed in the heavy rain without stopping, resting only in the evening. It was the most tiring day of his life for Shankar. Their clothes, their tents, their sacks of food, everything was soaked through and through. There was not a single dry piece of clothing left, not even a handkerchief.

Shankar felt extremely fatigued. The darkness of the day turned into the blackness of night; the mountains and the forests took on a fierce and an awe-inspiring look. Shankar wondered: *In this unknown land, in these virgin mountains, in this forest full of ferocious animals, what mirage was he chasing through this torrential rain? What diamond mine was he looking for? Did it even exist? Or was he going towards his death, unknowable at least for now, but certain in the end? What was Alvarez to him that he was following that old man like a disciple follows his teacher? Why did he follow Alvarez here? He did not want diamonds, he did not want the diamond mine.*

His mind went back to his beloved Bengal: the straw-roofed cottages of his village, the shadowed lanes through the gentle woods, the little river winding on its way, the familiar calls of the birds resting in the familiar trees. All these now appeared to be stuff of dreams, much more valuable than all the diamond mines in Africa.

His fatigue and dark feelings were allayed late at night when the rain stopped, the clouds cleared and the moon began to shine. He couldn't find words to describe the ethereal moonlit beauty his eyes met. He felt no longer on earth; vanished away was the land called Bengal as well as the continent called Africa. He was in a dreamlike state. He did not want to go anywhere, he did not yearn for diamonds, he did not want riches. He was now living in a different world, a white, shining paradise lit by the white, shining moon. The beauty of this world nobody had ever seen before. The solemn stillness of this world nobody had ever felt before. In this moonlit night, the huge Richtersveldt mountains and its forests looked still, self-absorbed, engrossed in meditation. Very few humans from the planet we call Earth had the rare good fortune of entering this world.

Later that night, he woke up all of a sudden. Alvarez was calling him urgently, 'Shankar, Shankar, get up, get the guns!'

'What's the matter? What's wrong?'

Then he heard it. Something was moving around the tent, as quietly as it could manage. The sound of its heavy breaths could be heard from inside the tent. The moon was about to set. The little moonlight that one could see lit up only the treetops; outside the tent the darkness was almost total. The fire had virtually died out, and the embers did not cast much light on the trees and bushes surrounding the camp.

Suddenly there was the rushing sound of a large, heavy creature running through the woods away from their camp. It was as if the animal that had been stalking them had come to realise that they were awake.

Whatever it might be, it was intelligent and had the ability of judgement.

Alvarez lit his torch and stepped outside the tent. Shankar followed. In the torchlight, they saw that the bushes and small trees on the north-eastern side of their camp had been crushed, as if run over by a heavy steamroller. Alvarez shot two rounds of his rifle in that direction – not in the hope of hitting something, but with the intention of scaring off any animal that might be lurking nearby.

There was complete silence all around.

On their way back to the tent, both saw a footprint on the soft earth right next to the fire, a few feet away from the front flap of their tent, almost eleven inches in length, with three distinct toes.

The animal was not scared of fire. Otherwise it wouldn't have dared to come so close to the tent. Shankar thanked his stars. If they had woken up even a minute later, the animal would not have hesitated to enter the tent and attack them. He didn't even try to imagine what would have been the result of such an attack.

Alvarez said, 'Shankar, you go back to sleep. I'll keep watch.'

Shankar said, 'No, no, I'll keep watch, you catch some sleep till daylight.'

Alvarez smiled and said, 'There's nothing you can do by staying awake, Shankar. Go back to sleep and take some rest. See, the clouds are gathering again. There's lightning in the air and it's going to rain soon. There's not much left of the night, so go back to sleep. I'll have some coffee to keep me awake.'

The rain came down again with daybreak. Again, a full torrential rain coming down in sheets, with thunder and lightning. It rained without any letup the whole morning, afternoon and through into the evening. It seemed to Shankar that the last days of the world had arrived and the God of Destruction himself had decided to wash away the world of its very existence. Even Alvarez didn't say a word about lifting camp and moving on.

It was five o'clock when the rain stopped. Unfortunately – from Shankar's point of view. Alvarez immediately ordered him to pack up their belongings and move forward on their journey again. The Bengali youth in Shankar was more than a little disappointed – here was a great chance to laze about through the evening, so why start their wanderings so late in the afternoon? They wouldn't lose anything by starting the next morning, would they? But to Alvarez, time meant nothing. They had to go on with their journey. The ticking of the clock or the cycle of seasons meant nothing to him.

Climbing up the moonlit forest, just washed clean by the rain, was a wonderful experience for Shankar. He had got into the rhythm of the climb, one foot forward, then the other, the first again, then again the other.... Suddenly Alvarez called from just behind him, 'Shankar, stop! Take a look, there!'

Alvarez was looking through his field glasses at the mountain on their left, lit up by the bright moonlight. Shankar took the glasses from Alvarez and looked at the peak. Yes, he could see the shallow slope, the long easy ledge below the peak. It wasn't very far away. Not more than two miles.

He looked at Alvarez and smiled. Alvarez smiled back. 'Did you see the saddle? We won't stop tonight. We'll go on to the saddle and camp there.'

What a folly he'd committed by joining this single-minded Portuguese fortune hunter on the wild search for a diamond mine! Shankar dragged his weary body and soul up the mountain, forcing himself on behind Alvarez. He knew that every exploration party, even consisting of just two men, had to have a leader, and that the leader's command was never to be questioned. This was an unwritten rule, and nobody ever broke it without risking lives of members of the team and, often, the very success of the exploration itself. Shankar knew this and was absolutely clear in his mind that he would follow it, whatever the cost.

After a non-stop trek through the night, they reached the saddle just as the day was breaking. Shankar had no strength left in his body, and couldn't have dragged himself even a single step further.

The saddle was at least three miles in length, with many ups and downs which made it difficult to cross. At some places, there was a steep climb of a couple of hundred feet, at others, one had to descend four or five hundred feet within one mile. The flat areas were all covered with dense trees and bushes. Shankar recognised erythrina, poinciana, soapberry bushes, wild ginger and a few others. The branches were loaded with strange and very beautiful orchids. Baboons and colobus monkeys were in abundance in this forest.

After descending for another two days, they reached the valley on the other side of the mountains. They had crossed the main range of the Richtersveldt! Shankar felt that the forests on this side of the mountains were, if it were possible, even more dense and impassable than those they had taken so much trouble to cross. The water vapour from the Atlantic Ocean coalesced into rain clouds. Some of these collided with the mountains in the Cameroons in West Africa and the rest were stopped in their journey by the plateaus of the gigantic Richtersveldt. Consequently, the forests in these valleys got a lot of rain, and this helped the trees and bushes to grow rapidly and without restraint.

Part 9

Chapter 1

THEY HAD BEEN WANDERING ABOUT IN THE HUGE FORESTED valley for more than fifteen days but had not found the mountain stream that Alvarez had described. They did find a few small streams, but Alvarez shook his head at each one of them, saying, 'This is not the one I am looking for.'

Shankar asked, 'Why don't you take a close look at the map?'

Alvarez said, 'How will the map help? My mind carries the most accurate picture of the stream and the valley through which it flows. If I see it, I will recognise it at once. This is not the right valley, no... this is not the right area through which the stream flows. We are in the wrong place.'

So, they had to continue with their search.

One month went by. The seasonal rains of West Africa started in the beginning of March. It was a dreadful time, and Shankar had had some experience of how dangerous it could be while traversing the Richtersveldt. The valley almost overflowed with the water borne down by the hundreds of mountain streams spawned by the rains. They were hard put to find a reasonably dry and safe place to pitch their tent. One night, a sudden shower in the mountains caused a little stream near their camp to swell up. Within minutes, the stream turned into a roaring torrent threatening their camp and their lives. Thanks to the alert Alvarez, they were able to save their belongings and themselves.

Time passed slowly. They did not seem to be getting any closer to the object of their search.

One day, Shankar had a close brush with death in the forest. A very strange thing happened to him.

Alvarez had warned him often to be very careful while travelling in forests such as these, reminding him time and again to always carry a loaded gun. He had also given him two extremely valuable pieces of advice: while travelling here, he must always wear his compass on his wrist; and, whenever he took a path, he must always leave a sign on the path or on the tree trunks, at regular intervals. So that, on his way back, he could follow these signs to the safety of the camp. Failure to follow these simple but crucial advices could mean danger, even death.

On that fateful day, Shankar had left the camp in the morning, following the tracks of a herd of springboks, and gone deep into the forest, quite far from the camp. *Deer meat would be a very welcome addition to their larder!* After hours of fruitless tracking, he sat down under a tree to rest. The tracking had been difficult and tiring.

Huge trees surrounded the little place and, around every tree, was the same type of creepers that clung to the tree trunks so tight and mimicked the colour of their hosts so closely that it was difficult to tell the difference between the trunks and the creepers. There was a little pool formed by a tiny brook, the banks of which were filled with blooming mariposa lily.

After resting for a while, Shankar suddenly felt a little uncomfortable. He couldn't tell what exactly the problem was but he felt that he should leave that place. At the same time, he felt a reluctance to get up and leave – the little glade was quite cool and comfortable, and he was tired. Perhaps he could stay just a little while longer, he thought.

Why this urgency to go away, and this aversion to do so? Was he falling sick, with malaria perhaps?

To get over this feeling of laziness, he took out a cheroot from his pack and lit it up. A sweet smell filled the air in the glade which he seemed to notice for the first time. It was pleasant and Shankar liked it very much. *Nice, restful place*, Shankar thought.

When he tried to put the matchbox back in his pocket, he was struck with another strange feeling: was the hand really his? It did not seem to obey him at all. While he wanted his hand to put the matchbox in his pocket and draw his pack near, it seemed to have a will of its own and no intention of obeying his brain.

Slowly his entire body was taken over by a restful and deliciously languorous feeling. *What's the point of his fruitless wandering? Why chase a mirage anymore? It was so much nicer spending the rest of his life in this glade, admiring nature, enjoying the beauty of his surroundings, lying thus against a tree trunk, resting his head on a little moss-covered rock.*

Once in a while, his mind told him that it was getting on towards afternoon, soon it would be sunset, and that it was high time he got up and went back to camp otherwise he could be in grave danger. Once he even tried to get up and leave but, the next moment, the languor took over his body. It was not fatigue or exhaustion; it was a delectable feeling of enjoyment, as if he had had too much of some excellent wine which made the mundane tasks of getting up and going back to his camp really trivial. This feeling of being slightly but enjoyably drunk made his body slow and unwilling to obey his mind.

Shankar lay down resting his head on a tree root of such a right size and height that nature couldn't have made him a better pillow had he ordered one. The fading sunlight playing in the leaves of the large cottonwood trees around him slowly became more and more indistinct. The hooting of an owl from the bole of a nearby tree became fainter and fainter.

Shankar had no idea what happened next.

It was quite late in the afternoon when Alvarez found Shankar's unconscious body amid the cottonwood trees. The first thought that came to his mind was that Shankar had been bitten by a snake. After a closer examination of his body, Alvarez was relieved that was not the case. A quick look at the trees and bushes in the glade made the whole thing clear to the experienced traveller. The creepers were of a highly poisonous variety. This was widespread in the forests of Africa and many tribes used the juice of this plant to poison their arrows. If breathed for a long time, the poison could lead to paralysis or even death.

Shankar was bedridden in the tent for three days. His body was swollen and his head felt like it would burst. He was constantly thirsty. No amount of water seemed to slake his thirst. Alvarez said, 'If I had discovered you the next morning instead of this afternoon, it would have been almost impossible to save you.'

Chapter 2

ONE DAY, WHILE RESTING ON THE BANKS OF A LITTLE RIVER, Shankar noticed something yellow. Alvarez, the expert prospector that he was, washed the sand of the river and found strains of gold. But he did not seem much excited. The quantity of gold was so little that the labour was just not worth it. He would get no more than three ounces of gold after washing one tonne of river sand!

Shankar felt otherwise. 'But that's still quite a lot. The price of three ounces of gold is pretty good.'

Due to his inexperience, he felt that their discovery was valuable. But the greater knowledge and experience of Alvarez said that if this was to be the outcome of their pains, their labour would be largely wasteful. Regretfully, Shankar had to bow to the greater expertise of Alvarez.

They wandered for another month, rather aimlessly as it seemed to Shankar. They would set up camp in one place for a couple of days and, after a detailed investigation of their surroundings, move to another.

They set up their tent in a new place in the forest. Shankar went out shooting some jungle fowl for food. When he returned in the evening, he found Alvarez smoking one of his cheroots with a very worried look on his face.

Shankar said, 'Alvarez, since you have not been able to find the place you are searching for, let's go back.'

Alvarez said, 'The river cannot have vanished off the face of earth. It is here somewhere in these forests, in these mountains. It has got to be here somewhere.'

Shankar said, 'Then why haven't we been able to find it?'

Alvarez said, 'Our search is faulty. Perhaps we are looking for it in the wrong place.'

Shankar said, 'Diego, we have been searching in these forests for the last six months! Where could we have gone astray?'

Alvarez looked grim and said, 'We have a big problem, Shankar. I did not tell you about this earlier, you would have been discouraged or even scared. Come, let me show you something.'

Shankar was very curious and not a little worried. He followed Alvarez into the forest, who stopped next to the trunk of a large tree. He said, 'Shankar, we came and camped here today, right?'

Shankar was surprised. 'Of course! What do you mean? We came here today. We haven't been here before.'

Alvarez called him nearer and said, 'All right, look at this tree trunk. What do you see?'

Shankar went closer and saw that on the soft bark of the tree were two letters carved into it with a knife – D A. The carving was not new; it looked to be more than a month old.

Shankar looked up at Alvarez in utter incomprehension. Alvarez explained, 'You haven't been able to understand this? I had carved these letters on this tree trunk about a month ago. Something has been bothering me for a while. It hasn't occurred to you – all forests look the same to you. Do you now realise what this means? We have been going round in circles in this forest. And when this happens, it's really dangerous and very difficult to break out of. But we have to, we must.'

Now Shankar understood their predicament. He said, 'You mean to say that we had been here about a month ago?'

'Exactly! This often happens in a very large forest or desert. It's called a "death circle". About a month ago, I had realised that we have perhaps fallen into a death circle. To test my hypothesis, I had carved those two letters in the bark of that tree. This afternoon, while I had gone into the forest, I suddenly noticed these two letters.'

Shankar said, 'But what happened to our compass? How can we be going around in circles while our compass is working?'

Alvarez said, 'I am not sure if that is working. You remember the big thunderstorm we went through while crossing the Richtersveldt range? I suspect that the lightning had affected the magnetism of the compass needle.'

'So, it's now useless? It doesn't work anymore?'

'Yes, I am convinced that it doesn't.'

Shankar now fully understood their plight. The maps were wrong; the compass was useless. And to top it all, they'd fallen into a death circle in this huge, impenetrable forest. No human beings close by whom they could call upon for help; not much food left; not much drinking water either. The water from the mountain streams carried various minerals and bacteria, so could not be trusted for drinking. The only certainty was that of a mysterious, perhaps even violent death. Death that had claimed Jim Carter, who had come to these accursed forests in search of jewels. Death would now perhaps claim the two of them as well.

But Alvarez was not one to be dismayed by such a turn of events. Day after day, he trudged on through the forests, driving Shankar with him. The latter couldn't anyway distinguish directions in the forest and, after hearing about the death circle, he had lost that sense completely.

About three days later, they came to a place which looked completely new to them. A smaller range of the main Richtersveldt mountain range had branched off to the north at right angles. It appeared to be at least four thousand feet high; to the west, a high peak was covered with heavy clouds. The valley in between the mountains was about three miles in width and covered with very dense forest.

The trees in the forest were in three or four layers. Right at the top were parasites, moss and lichens. In the middle were huge trees and creepers. At the bottom were bushes and smaller plants. Sunlight could not penetrate into the thick tree cover.

Alvarez set up camp just on the edge of this dense forest. Drinking coffee outside their tent in the evening, they took stock of their situation, and contemplated what they should do next. Their food was finished, they had run out of sugar quite some time ago, and it looked as if their stock of coffee would get over in a few days. They only had some flour left since they used it sparingly. This was all they had carried from the civilised world. From now on, their main source of food would have to be the meat of the animals they killed. Even here they needed to be careful – they were carrying a limited number of cartridges and could not afford to waste even a single shot.

While talking, Shankar looked at the mountain peak they'd seen in the morning, when it was covered with clouds. Now, the clouds had cleared completely and he noticed that the peak had a very strange shape, as if someone had taken a bite from one side of an ice-cream cone.

Alvarez said, 'From here, Bulawayo or Salisbury should be about four or five hundred miles in the south-easterly direction. On the way, there's two hundred miles of desert. If you go west, the Atlantic coast should be about three hundred miles. But we have to cross the very dangerous and thick forests of Portuguese West Africa. Let's forget about that…we can't go in that direction. The only option left for us is that either you or I go to Salisbury or Bulawayo and bring back tinned food and cartridges. We also need a new compass.'

Much later, Shankar thanked Alvarez for these words, and his guardian angel for making him pay attention to this conversation. The names of those two large cities – Salisbury and Bulawayo – and their direction and rough distances remained in his mind in later days.

They were really tired that night, so they turned in early to prepare for the next day.

Part 10

Chapter 1

$\mathcal{L}$ATE AT NIGHT, SHANKAR WOKE UP FROM A DEEP SLEEP. There was a dull noise coming from outside; something was happening somewhere in the forest. He couldn't put his finger on it and that made him anxious. Diego Alvarez was also sitting awake in his bed, listening intently, trying to identify the noise and understand what was going on.

Shankar was about to light his torch and step out of the tent but Alvarez stopped him. 'I have told you so many times not to leave your tent in a hurry like this, especially when there can be danger outside! And why are you going out without your gun?'

It was totally black outside the tent and, in the light of their torches, they could see the reason for the noise – hundreds of animals, big and small, were running pell-mell at the top of their speed out of the forest, towards the hills in the east. Hyenas, baboons, wild buffaloes, monkeys, apes… A couple of leopards almost ran into them in their haste. The animals ran past the two friends and their tent without paying the slightest of attention to them. A large tribe of colobus monkeys ran past them, with the females holding their babies onto their chests. *If they didn't get out of the way, they would be run over by the mad stampede!*

Why were they running like this? What were they running away from? Even Alvarez had never witnessed a sight like this.

Suddenly, a new sound was added to the noise of the stampede – a deep, dull, thudding sound, like a distant but continuous thunder, as if thousands of bass drums were being beaten somewhere far away.

Shankar and Alvarez stared at each other in the dim light of their torches, their eyes asking a question which neither could answer. Alvarez screamed, 'Shankar, light up the fire quickly! Otherwise the wild animals will run all over us and our tent. Let's go, hurry!'

The stampede increased manifold; now the birds too were deserting their nests and joining the mad desperate flight.

A huge springbok almost grazed past Shankar, but the thought of shooting it for food didn't even strike them. They were too dumbstruck to think or act with reason.

Shankar turned to ask Alvarez something. At the same moment, it appeared to him that the final moment of the world had arrived. The earth lurched and shivered beneath their feet, the sound of a thousand bolts of lightning struck their ears and it seemed that the sky had split into tiny pieces. Somehow they managed to pick themselves up from the ground. Alvarez shouted, 'Earthquake!' And then the darkness was rudely pierced by the light of some fifty thousand floodlights going up simultaneously.

They turned to look at the mountain tops. The strange one they had noticed a few days ago was on fire, a fire so huge that lit up the sky in that direction all the way to the horizon. The monstrous red flame seemed to climb up more than two thousand feet into the sky.

At the same time they smelled something which was frighteningly unfamiliar – the horrible smell of sulphur had befouled the whole atmosphere.

Alvarez looked at the sky and exclaimed in fear, 'A volcano! *Santa Anna Grazia de Cordova.*'

What a dangerously beautiful sight! They couldn't take their eyes off the flaming mountain and the orange skies. If a million flares and a million Diwali torches had been all lit up together, it would not have matched this beauty. The flame on the peak dipped a little from time to time but quickly flared up as if somebody had thrown more fuel into the fire. And, throughout, there was the sound of thousands of bombs going off every moment.

They just couldn't keep standing on the unsteady earth. Shankar somehow entered the tent. A tiny creature, looking like an Alsatian puppy, sat shivering on his bed, staring back at the torchlight, frozen with fright by the noise around him. Alvarez said, 'It's a wolf cub. Let it be, it's really scared – don't hurt it.'

They had never seen an active volcano before. They really had no idea of how great a danger they were in. But they didn't have to wait long for the answer. Alvarez had barely finished speaking when they heard a heavy object hitting the ground outside their tent. They ran out and saw that a huge, red-hot stone had fallen on a bush a few yards away, and the bush sprang into flames immediately. A few other stones fell nearby, and the trees and undergrowth caught fire. Alvarez shouted, 'Shankar, we have to get away, right now! Pack up quickly – as fast as you can!'

While they were lifting camp, a few more stones fell around them, and the smell of sulphur got stronger and more suffocating.

Chapter 2

*T*HEY RAN AND RAN. FOR TWO HOURS OR MORE, THEY carried and dragged their belongings eastwards down the mountain. The smell of sulphur pervaded the air all the way to the valley. A little while after they stopped to catch their breath, flaming stones started falling around them. They had to climb out of the valley, up the mountain on the other side, somehow pushing through the dense forest lit up by the fiery skies.

At dawn, they were panting for breath under a tree some two-and-a-half thousand feet up the slope of the mountain on the other side of the valley.

With sunrise, the volcanic eruption became less dramatic, but the sound of falling rocks seemed to increase. In addition, the sky started raining a very fine ash, which soon covered all the leaves and branches with a thick layer of grey.

The eruption continued throughout the day and, at night, the terrible flaming light returned. The forest and the sky were on fire. The only relief was that the falling of rocks had decreased slightly. But the red fiery clouds around the volcano were just as bright as before.

Somehow they curled up on the ground to catch a little sleep. But not for long. Late at night, they were woken up by the sound of a huge explosion. They turned to the volcano peak and noticed that it had been blown away completely. The valley below them was covered with flaming rocks and ash. Alvarez was grazed slightly by a falling rock, their tent caught fire, and some of the branches of the tree under which they were sheltering also caught fire.

They hurried up the slope trying to find a safer place, away from danger. Shankar wondered whether anybody else besides themselves had seen such an incredible natural event. If they had not been witness to this incredible show of Mother Nature's powers, they wouldn't have ever believed such a story, and now that they had seen it, he was sure that nobody would believe them when they told their story. Perhaps nobody knew of the existence of the volcano here in the wild mountains of the Richtersveldt range.

Next morning, they could clearly see the peak of the volcano, which looked it had melted from the side like a candle is by its flame when caught in a breeze.

Alvarez looked at the map. 'The map doesn't mark this as a volcano. Perhaps it had been dormant for many decades. However, the native name mentioned in the map is very interesting.'

'What's it?'

'It's written here – Oldonyo Lengai. In the ancient Zulu language, this means "The Bed of the Fire God." Obviously, the ancient inhabitants of this land knew that this was a volcano. Possibly, it had not erupted for a couple of hundred years, and Europeans did not know about its nature.'

The Indian in Shankar prompted him to genuflect facing the mountain. 'My prayers, O Rudradev, my prayers to you! You have given me the opportunity to see your powers, and you have protected me from the destruction you have wrought. Thank you, and my prayers to you again! A thousand diamond mines, a million diamonds – they are all nothing compared to the beauty and power you have allowed me to glimpse. All my toils and troubles are worth it. My prayers to you!'

Chapter 3

ALVAREZ DID NOT THINK IT SAFE TO CAMP SO CLOSE TO THE volcano. The phrase 'baptism of fire' could take a most unpleasant meaning for them! They were still too close for comfort to the still-smoking caldera of Oldonyo Lengai. So, one afternoon they packed up and started moving westwards, where the forest was still intact, virtually untouched by the flames, lava and the rockfalls from the volcano. The vegetation was, if anything, even denser than the forest they had travelled in earlier. Through the trees and bushes flowed myriad mountain streams and brooks – none of which were familiar to Alvarez.

After a few days, they arrived at a more open area in the forest, surrounded by hillocks of different sizes, formed of chalk and granite, pockmarked by caves, small and large. This place looked a little different from the other places they had visited in the Richtersveldt Mountains. Though the forest here was not as dense, the trees were larger and, on all sides, there were hills and caves.

They climbed a small granite hill and camped for the night. There was something about the place that made Shankar feel uncomfortable – something deep inside him told him that this was not a good place; there was a definite but indefinable sense of danger. Neither could he explain this to himself, nor could he bring himself to express this feeling to Alvarez.

A few days later, Alvarez told him, 'We are wasting our time here, Shankar. We are still going round in circles in the forest. You remember the tree I had shown you earlier? The one with the initials D A carved on the bark? I saw this tree today. But you know that for the last fifteen days we have moved in a westerly direction, away from the forest we had travelled in earlier. So, how could we have come to the same tree today? I don't understand it!'

Shankar said, 'What do we do now?'

'There is something we can do. I will climb to the top of a large tree and fix our location after sighting the stars. That is the best thing to do. You will stay in the tent.'

Shankar was puzzled. If they were going round in circles, how did they reach this area of hillocks and caves? He had never visited this place before – of that he was quite certain. Alvarez had said that after seeing the initials carved on the tree, he had not tried to travel eastwards from there at all. If he had done so even for a couple of miles, they would have reached this tree.

That night, Shankar lay in his bed in the tent reading Bankim Chandra's *Rajsingha*. This was the only Bengali book that he had managed to bring with him when he left home. Even though he had read it a thousand times, it still engrossed him.

India was so far away; places like Chittor, Mewar, other places in the Rajputana, and the fights between the Moghuls and the Rajputs – all these seemed so unreal, sitting in the middle of this huge dense forest in Africa.

Suddenly, Shankar heard the sound of footsteps near the tent. *Alvarez is coming back after his examination of the stars* was the first thought that crossed Shankar's mind. But there was something different about the sound of these footsteps. They were not the natural, confident steps of a man who knows where he is going, but it was as if somebody was limping and dragging himself with pain and difficulty with feet wrapped in cloth bags. Silently, Shankar reached out and grabbed the Winchester repeater, and sat pointing it at the tent door, taking care not to make the slightest noise. The sound outside the tent stopped, but started again a few seconds later on the southern side. This time, Shankar could hear the sound of a large animal breathing, just like the one he had heard on another night some weeks ago while crossing the mountain.

The memory of that night scared him and he lost control over himself. He cocked the rifle and shot in the direction of the sound...once...twice....

Almost immediately, he heard Alvarez's revolver firing twice in response. Obviously, Alvarez thought that Shankar was in trouble – he was not the kind to shoot without purpose. He was probably hurrying back to the camp to help Shankar.

Now there was total silence around the tent. The four shots had probably scared off the animal. Shankar thought of going out and lighting his torch. He wanted to signal to Alvarez of possible danger and tell him not to come to the camp when suddenly, from a few hundred yards away in the forest, he heard the sound of a revolver firing twice and a muffled scream.

Shankar rushed in that direction. Some distance away, he found a large tree, under which lay Alvarez. Shankar shuddered in dismay and fear at what he saw in the torchlight: Alvarez's whole body was bathed in blood, his head was bent at an unnatural angle, his coat was severely torn.

Shankar sat down next to him, cradled his head in his arms and gently called, 'Alvarez! Alvarez!'

Alvarez did not respond. His lips moved with a lot of effort, as if he was trying very hard to say something. He looked at Shankar, but there was no recognition, no spark of intelligence, no energy in his eyes.

Somehow, Shankar carried him to the tent. After gently forcing some water down his throat, he tried to take the torn coat off Alvarez's body. It came off soaked in blood. Shankar saw to his horror that a huge chunk of flesh near Alvarez's left shoulder was torn off and his back was deeply scratched. It looked as if a very strong animal had repeatedly scratched and torn open his back with sharp claws and teeth.

Now he remembered having noticed pugmarks under the tree where he found Alvarez – pugmarks that showed the same three toes in each foot.

Chapter 4

$\mathcal{S}$HANKAR SOMEHOW ENDURED THAT NIGHT. THERE WAS NO sound, no response, not even a sign of consciousness from Alvarez throughout. At dawn, Alvarez suddenly seemed to regain some of his wits. He looked around blankly, and then at Shankar as if this was the first time he was seeing him. He closed his eyes and again lapsed into unconsciousness. Some hours later, he started muttering to himself in Portuguese, his mother tongue, of which Shankar could not understand a single word. In the afternoon, he opened his eyes again and suddenly looked at Shankar. It seemed that the old Alvarez was back. He recognised Shankar immediately and asked him in English, 'Shankar, why haven't you got ready yet? Let's go, pack up the tent and our belongings, and let's go.' He waved his hands, pointing in no specific direction. 'Shankar, I can see a king's ransom hidden in that cave – over there. You can't see it, but I can, I have just seen it. Let's move now, let's not waste any more time. Hurry! Hurry!'

Those were the last words spoken by Alvarez.

Shankar sat like stone, in complete silence. He lost count of the hours. Afternoon gave way to evening and the trees and bushes slowly faded into the gathering darkness. Soon, it was totally black inside the tent and outside.

Shankar suddenly realised it was night. He quickly started the campfire, brought out both the rifles, loaded them, put some more bullets in his pocket, and sat up the whole night next to Alvarez's body, with his guns aimed at the door flap.

Later that evening, it started raining. It rained as if the gods wanted to wash the world clean of all dirt. Everything in the camp was soaked in rainwater. But Shankar did not pay any attention to his condition or that of the camp. He was lost in thought, reliving the last few months that he had spent with Alvarez.

In these months, he had come to know and love Alvarez like his own father. He had come to admire the man for his courage, his single-mindedness, his strength and his dedication. The man had fascinated him. And he knew that Alvarez loved him like his own son.

But above all, Shankar was wondering about the way he died. He was killed by the strange creature that the natives in the village had warned them of. He had died the same death as his old friend, Jim Carter.

As the night progressed, Shankar started to feel really afraid. Somewhere out there in the forest, maybe right outside his tent, was waiting the deliverer of a cruel and violent death. Nobody knew when and where he would strike. Shankar must stay awake the whole night. If he dozed off even for a second, he might fall prey to the killer. He must stay awake, whatever it took.

This was the worst night in his entire life – one he would have loved to forget but was condemned to remember forever. The sound of the rain falling on each branch, each twig, each leaf; the sound of the storm throughout the night – they drowned out all the other sounds of the forest. From time to time came the crashing sound of branches breaking off from the trees and falling to the ground. Also the noise of large trees that had reached the end of their existence and crashed onto the ground, taking other trees with them. The tree trunks were like ghosts – black, occasionally made visible by the lightning of the storm.

In the middle of this nightmare, Shankar was alone, completely alone. The dead body of his greatest friend lay in front of him. He must keep his calm. Otherwise he would die of fright. He had to be brave, and the thought of his two guns gave him some courage. He brought out his Winchester and the Mannlicher, Alvarez's favourite weapon; he made sure that the magazines of both were fully loaded. He put two belts of cartridges around his waist and shoulders. He was now ready for any beast that tried to enter the tent. Not a single animal could trouble him now that he had his two trusted guns.

Sometimes fear and danger makes a man brave. Shankar just could not afford to be afraid and stayed awake all night. In the grey light of dawn, he noticed that the rain had dropped off quite a bit. He buried Alvarez under a large tree, made a rough cross with two branches and pushed it down hard on the grave as the last sign of where his dearest friend had been laid to rest.

While clearing up the camp, Shankar came upon a few personal papers of Alvarez. He found a diploma from the college of mining in Oporto – Alvarez had passed the final examination with distinction. Shankar was not surprised since he had long ago understood that Alvarez was a man of considerable learning and education, not like other wanderers who searched for fame and fortune armed only with guns and luck.

Far away from his native Portugal, far away from any town or village, in the middle of the deepest and most dangerous forest in Africa, Alvarez had come to his journey's end. His search for diamonds, gold, silver and other riches was finally over. But he would not have regretted that – he was not like other fortune hunters. He loved the journey for its own sake; all the riches of the richest kings on earth would not have been able to hold him back.

It was a fitting grave for a courageous traveller. The huge trees, the kings of the forest, would provide shade upon his last resting place. Lions, gorillas, hyenas and other animals would make sure that nobody disturbed his peace. And, above all, the huge Richtersveldt Mountains would forever keep watch on the spot where Alvarez finally lay his weary body to rest.

Part 11

Chapter 1

*S*HANKAR SPENT THE NEXT DAY AND NIGHT IN THE SAME forest camp. Somehow he felt a reluctance to move on. But finally he forced himself to get moving and break up camp. If he wanted to stay alive, he had to pack up, leave, traverse the forest and the mountains, and reach a place of human habitation. Sitting idle in the forest was a certain invitation to death.

But where would he go? He had never been in these parts before and was not sure he could read the maps that Alvarez had left behind.

Suddenly, he remembered the name Salisbury. Alvarez had once mentioned that magical word, *nearly six hundred miles from here in a south-easterly direction.*

Salisbury – the capital of Southern Rhodesia. That was where he would go; somehow, some day he would reach there. He remembered an incident from his childhood: the local priest was reading his horoscope, and he had pronounced that Shankar would live till a ripe old age. He took comfort from this memory. He would not die in this godforsaken place; he would get out of here and reach safety.

Shankar brought out all the maps he could find in the camp. There was a Forest Survey map of the Portuguese Government; a map from 1873 of the coastal districts made by the Royal Marine

Survey, another of the Richtersveldt area made by the famous traveller Sir Filippo de Filippi and, of course, a much-abused sketch map drawn by Alvarez and signed by Jim Carter. Shankar had never paid much attention to understand and read these maps while Alvarez was alive, and now his life depended entirely on how he made use of them. He had to find out on the map where he was currently, and then find viable means of escape from the forests and reach human habitation.

After much study, Shankar realised that none of the maps, except the sketch by Alvarez and Carter, could throw much light on where he was right now. The maps had not surveyed the Richtersveldt region with any degree of thoroughness. But the sketch map had its limitations for a different reason: while he was certain that it was accurate, the creators had used signs and symbols only they could understand, just in case the map fell into wrong hands, and others found and laid claim to the riches hidden in the mountains!

Shankar now had to come to the conclusion that the maps were, by and large, useless for him. If he wanted to get out of here, he would have to depend on his wits and his luck.

On the fourth day after Alvarez's death, Shankar struck camp. He laid a garland of wild flowers on Alvarez's grave and started travelling eastward.

Travellers in Africa often refer to a skill they call 'bush craft'. It is a skill every traveller has to learn and master to venture in the wild forests or grasslands of Africa – ignorance can lead to death. Shankar had learnt quite a lot from Alvarez, but he couldn't call himself a master by any means. Now, he had to depend on what he had learnt. There would be nobody to train him; and if he failed, there would be one more shining white skeleton in these forests.

He crossed a few hillocks. The forests changed in appearance as he travelled east. Sometimes they were really dense, sometimes lighter. There were large trees everywhere. Shankar knew that if he reached the elephant grass, he could be sure he had come out of the forests, since elephant grass and tussock grass don't grow in deep forests. So far he had not come across any – only huge trees and a lot of dense undergrowth.

By the end of the first day, he was in an even denser forest. While leaving his camp, he had left most of his belongings behind. All that he had taken with him was his rifles, as much ammunition as he could carry, water bottles, torches, maps, compass, his watch, blanket, some medicines, and a hammock. The tent too he had to abandon; although it was very light, he thought he would find it troublesome to carry around for a long time.

He strung up the hammock between two trees, at quite some distance from the ground. After lighting a large fire, he sat in the hammock the whole night cradling his rifles. Sleep was impossible; even if he felt sleepy, the mosquitoes made sure he remained awake. In the late evening, a leopard started loitering around the camp, obviously with intent. In the darkness, his eyes were lit up by the campfire, which vanished as the leopard went into the long grass every time Shankar trained his torch on him. A few minutes later, when Shankar switched off the torch, the leopard appeared at the edge of the camp, staring at Shankar. This clever animal really scared him – the beast could jump onto the hammock or the tree, and attack him if he ever let his guard down for even a fraction of a second.

In addition, there were other strange noises from the strange forest. Late at night, he must have fallen asleep for just a few minutes when he was woken up, with a start, by the sound of children laughing. *Where would children come from at this hour, in this forest? What was going on?*

He quickly remembered that there was a species of baboons in these deep forests, whose calls sounded very much like the laughter of small children. Alvarez had told him about this some time ago.

Chapter 2

$\mathcal{N}$EXT MORNING, HE PACKED UP HIS BELONGINGS AND continued on his journey. He was almost flying blind like an aviator whose instruments were malfunctioning. He was travelling through the forest without any sense of direction, depending entirely on luck. He was lost in the forest, with a compass which did not work.

On the fifth day, he stopped to rest at the foot of a hill. From a huge cave nearby, a thin mountain stream wended its merry way through stones and into the forest.

He had never seen such a large cave before. He felt quite safe and really curious. So he left his belongings in a nearby bush and went in to explore the cave. As he went deeper into it, he lit up his torch and began to step further very cautiously. Soon he came to a place where the path branched into two. In the torchlight, Shankar saw that the roof was very high, and stalactites of calcium carbonate hung from the ceiling like chandeliers.

The walls of the cave were wet and, in many places, Shankar could feel thin streams of water flowing down the walls. He took the right fork, and the thin entrance soon widened into a considerably larger cave. The ground was no longer made of stone, but of damp earth. In the torchlight, he saw that the cave was triangular in shape, and there was another entrance at another point in the triangle.

Shankar went in through this new entrance, and got into a thin gulley with high granite walls on both sides. He curiously went down this winding little gulley for quite some distance.

After about a couple of hours of this aimless wandering, Shankar turned to get back to his belongings in the bush and prepare for the night. But he could not find the triangular cave. He found the narrow corridor from which he had come, but he just could not find the cave through which he would have to find his way out into the forest clearing.

Strange! he thought. He knew the cave so well, so why couldn't he find it? He now noticed that the narrow gulley had little alleyways branching out at various places, and he was very possibly quite lost.

LOST. The very word churned his stomach. He sat down and breathed deeply, fighting the growing fear. He could not afford to panic; he just could not afford to get frightened. He had to keep calm and think through this new danger and find a way out – if he wished to survive. He remembered what Alvarez had told him so many times: in an unfamiliar territory, he must keep marking signs of his progress, so that he could follow the same signs in order to get back. He had forgotten this very basic advice, and now he had to suffer the consequences.

To top it all, he could not keep his torch lighted all the time, in case the batteries ran out. The cave system was pitch-dark. Without his torch, he would not be able to move even one foot, let alone find his way out.

By his watch, it was now seven o'clock in the evening. The torch batteries were clearly running out of juice; he could use them only intermittently now. The air in the cave was hot, stuffy and damp, and his water bottle was lying outside. The cave did have water – the thin streamlets seeping down the walls were definitely drinkable, only it was slightly salty in taste and there wasn't much of it. He had to lick the water off the walls.

It was now half past seven. Then eight, nine, ten…Shankar was still to find his way out of the cave. The torch had been in use since three in the afternoon and now it gave out only a feeble light. Shankar felt as if his own life depended on the torch. Without its thin little light, he would not be able to work his way out of this hellish cave; not even Alvarez would have been able to do so in complete darkness.

He switched off the torch for a while and sat on a piece of stone. He needed to think clearly; he needed not to panic. If he had a source of light, he felt sure he would be able to get out quickly. He knew that in his stupidity he had forgotten to bring more batteries with him but there was no point in looking back at things he had not done. He had to look forward to what he could do from now on to save himself.

For a while, he thought that he should sleep where he was. The next moment, he realised that the cave was so dark and bereft of natural light that it must be night forever inside.

After resting for a while, he went ahead groping blindly along the walls. According to his watch, it was now morning, which was not much of good news – the cave system remained engulfed in total darkness. Shankar was feeling as if he would faint with hunger and thirst. He felt that this cave was where his bones would be put to eternal rest; the Gods of Africa were not satisfied with the life of Alvarez as sacrifice, they wanted him as well.

He must have spent three days and three nights wandering about the cave. He was no longer sure about the time he had spent inside. He could just about make some assessment based on his watch. He had eaten up the inner soles of his boots and had started on the covers. He could not find a single rat or cockroach or even a scorpion which he could kill and eat. He felt that he was slowly losing his mind, but he was driven by one single idea – he had to get out of this cave somehow, somehow he had to see daylight again. That was why he was pushing his weak body along the walls of the cave system, looking for the way out to the grass clearing. Even if he had to do that till the moment of his death, he would not stop searching.

Chapter 3

HE MUST HAVE FALLEN ASLEEP; OR AGAIN, HE MIGHT HAVE passed out.

When he woke up, he felt as exhausted as when he'd fallen asleep, he didn't know when. The watch showed twelve o'clock – noon or midnight, there was no way he could tell.

He dragged himself upright and started walking again, hugging the wall on his right. A little distance ahead, he thought he saw something like a large piece of stone standing in his way. He switched on the torch just once. He saw that another wall of the cave blocked most of his way, standing out at right angle to the wall he was hugging.

Suddenly, he stood up, his whole body and mind on full alert. Wasn't that the sound of flowing water? Of course, it was the sound of water! Indeed it was the sound of a brook flowing over pebbles. He stopped to listen more carefully – yes, it sounded like it was coming from the other side of the wall which was blocking his way. He laid his ear against the wall. He was right. He had to get to this brook – that was surely his way to safety!

He searched for any hole in the blocking wall. He had no tools to dig a way through, so unless there was a natural way to reach the other side, the brook was only as good as a chimera. After a careful search, he found it! The Gods of Africa were kind to him after all. There was indeed a narrow path to the other side.

He had to crawl across the opening and, on the other side, he felt water – ice-cold flowing water! With half his body still in the narrow opening, he felt upwards to touch the ceiling. He couldn't feel any. Thankfully, there was space enough for him to stand upright. Carefully, he dragged himself out of the passageway, and stood up in a stream of water which flowed over his feet and what remained of his shoes.

Thank God! Now that he had found the stream, safety could not be too far away.

He knelt down and drank his fill of the clear water. After a while, he switched on his torch to study the way in which the stream flowed. He had to memorise this – the mouth of the cave would always be downstream, and he would not be able to use his torch for much longer.

He switched off the torch. In the total darkness, he would have to find his way out by feel and touch. Slowly, he went forward, studying the flow of the stream at every step, following every twist and turn of the little brook.

At one place, he felt that the stream broke up into three or four smaller streams going in different directions. Which way should he go? Which stream should he follow? He switched on the torch to study the streams.

He remembered Alvarez's advice. He must leave signs of his progress, so that he didn't get lost again.

In the torchlight, he noticed that the whole floor of the cave passage was strewn with small round pebbles over which the streams burbled. He filled his pockets with these pebbles, and followed each little stream to see if it led to the exit. He placed two pebbles side by side on the side of each stream, and each time the stream broke into two or three parts, he made a 'S' sign with pebbles. Every time he reached a dead end or where the stream vanished in some crack in the floor or the wall, he would trace his tracks back and collected his pebbles back.

After spending quite a lot of time, he realised he was back where he had started. He had gone down every little stream he could find and had not found a way out of the cave. He was bitterly disappointed, but he had to keep up his spirits if he wanted to get out of this alive.

Once, he really got the scare of his life. His feet touched something very cold and switching on the torch he found that he had almost stepped onto a huge python, lying all coiled up in the water! The python, disturbed in its rest, raised its head and stared into the torchlight, its eyes like a pair of lifeless beads. Still, the dim torchlight dazzled the snake, which probably saved Shankar's life. A hungry python is a fearsome beast, and many human lives have been lost in the coils of these creatures. One could be attacked by lions and tigers and still live to tell the tale; escape from the crushing coils of a python was unheard of.

Now Shankar felt a lot more worried travelling in the dark. Fate had saved him once from the python; surely, he would be taxing its patience by asking them to save him one more time! But he couldn't stand still at one place, he had to go on searching for escape.

He marked the place where he had stepped onto the stream with a large cross made out of little pebbles. He followed the one he thought was the main stream, exploring every single rivulet that branched out. At times, the ceiling came down so low that he had to bend down like an arthritic old man. At other times, he crawled along on hands and knees.

At one place, he switched on his torch just to get his bearings –

and yes, this was the triangular cave. He couldn't be wrong, he must not be wrong. This indeed was the triangular cave which he had lost, the search of which had sent him on a journey all the way to death's door and back.

A little later, he found a tiny window framed in the darkness, a little above his head. Through the window, far away, he could see a few stars, twinkling invitingly in the darkness. He was safe! That was the mouth of the cave. He would very shortly be out of here, in the safer surroundings of the forest clearance, where he had left his belongings. Finally!

When he stepped out of the cave, it was three in the morning. Lying in the little forest clearing, he looked up at the sky, and revelled in the sight of the stars shining in the clear night sky. He thanked all the Gods he could call upon for his miraculous escape.

And then, thankfully, his exhausted body could not hold out any more, and he fell into a dreamless, blissful sleep.

Part 12

1

Chapter 1

*H*E WOKE TO A BRIGHT, CLEAR MORNING. THE SUN, SHINING in the blue sky, lit up branches and leaves on the treetops, and sunlight filtered through them to warm the ground on which Shankar had been sleeping.

He sat up thinking for a while. He had to leave this place, peaceful and cheerful though it was, but had too many unpleasant memories. He had promised himself that he would go to Salisbury somehow. He must leave now. He felt in his pockets – he still had a few of those small, round pebbles he had picked up inside the cave. He kept them as a souvenir of his narrow escape. He ate a frugal breakfast and made his way through the forest, going south-east by his reckoning.

The next day, a few patches of elephant grass appeared in small clearings in the forest and, the same evening, the forest ended and the grasslands began. At night, Shankar studied his maps very carefully for a long time. The grassland that faced him was spread, according to the map, almost three hundred miles across, to the banks of the Zambezi River. He had to cross this immense savannah to reach his goal. However, some part of this journey would have to be through the infamous Kalahari Desert – an uninhabited, waterless land spanning some one hundred and seventy-five miles, devoid of paths, food or any means of survival. Alvarez had made some notes from a military map: there was just one, only one safe way to cross the Kalahari, which lay in the north-eastern corner of the desert. Attempting any other way was to invite death. The map called it 'The Land of Thirst', appropriately enough!

Once he reached Rhodesia, his journey would be a lot easier. There were large villages, settlements and towns in this land, and he could make his way to Salisbury with much greater safety.

The route was clear but very difficult. Shankar remembered that Alvarez had talked about going down this route, alone, to Salisbury, buy food and ammunition and come back to Shankar's camp. If a sixty-two-year-old man was so confident of undertaking this long and difficult journey, there was no way Shankar would back out of it.

However, sheer bravado was one thing; reaching Salisbury something else altogether. Success, and indeed, survival would depend largely on knowledge and experience. Both of these Shankar lacked. He could not read a map with as much expertise as Alvarez. In the military map of the Kalahari Desert, two ponds of water had been marked out. Shankar had often watched Alvarez, sitting by the light of a campfire, work out complicated mathematical calculations involving latitudes and longitudes of the ponds, the magnetic north and true north. He had been curious but had never taken the trouble to learn how to do those and other calculations from the map. And now, of course, it was too late anyway.

So, he had to depend only on his courage and luck. Fate had been kind to him so far. He commended his future to his gods and prepared for the long and difficult journey.

Chapter 2

$\mathcal{W}$ITHIN TWO DAYS OF HIS JOURNEY, HE WAS IN TROUBLE. He was completely lost. He cursed himself for not learning more from Alvarez when he had the opportunity. Any knowledgeable and experienced person would have been able to find at least one of the ponds marked in the map. Shankar had passed within three miles of this pond, without even realising it. His water was finishing fast, and he had to find a new source really soon.

What a journey this was turning out to be! A wasted arid land, with hills and mountains scattered among the plains, some cacti bushes and euphorbia plants, and piles of granite here and there – this land offered the wayfarer no food, no water, no companionship, since no man lived here, and no man in his right mind would want to cross it. Emptiness filled every day, day after day. In this land bereft of landmarks, you travelled only towards the horizon, and the horizon went away from you as you went closer to it. You had only the fireball overhead called the Sun and the fiery sand grains below your feet as your constant companions. The sun rose, the sun set, the stars appeared, the stars disappeared, the moon rose, the moon set, the sun rose again, the sun set again – there was nothing to break the monotony. It was impossible for Shankar to keep track of how much of the three hundred miles he had already crossed.

Not that the land was completely lifeless. During the day, the lizards of the desert called out to each other; at night, the crickets gave him company. Sometimes, he saw birds which he hunted for food. Once he killed a buzzard, and had to force himself to eat the tough, sour meat. On some days, he was lucky when he could catch hill scorpions. Their sting meant death, but they were really good eating!

After two days of search, he finally found a pool of water sheltered by some rocks. The water was deep red in colour, dead insects floated on the surface, some animal lay dead – bloated and rotting – on the opposite bank. But still, it was water! Shankar drank his fill and filled his bottles with this red liquid. He had no idea when he would find another source of water again in his journey.

Days passed. Shankar had very little idea of how much time had passed – it could be days, weeks, months, even years. All he knew was that he was walking and walking forward, ever forward. He walked through the evenings and early mornings to avoid the heat of the day. Little did he know where he was going; all he knew was that he had to keep on going forward. If he kept on doing so, he would reach Salisbury, then India, then his beloved little village in Bengal.

He now entered the real Kalahari Desert. Its first sight made him blanch: *how can any man ever survive this fiery plain, let alone cross it!* Sand, sand and even more sand; plains, hills and valleys, all made of copper-coloured sand, burning in the heat of the day, shining so bright that it hurt his eyes. At the edge of this deadly plain, Shankar's thermometer recorded a temperature of 127° Fahrenheit in the shade.

This was the desert he had to cross if he wanted to get to safety, and then home. And he had to do it alone.

Before stepping onto this terrible land, Shankar spent an entire evening studying his maps. The only way he should attempt to cross was via the north-east corner; any other route would be sheer suicide, and a very unpleasant way of so doing, since he would certainly die of thirst. There was absolutely no water except the three natural water holes marked on the maps: thirty, seventy and ninety miles from where he was. These were in little cracks in the plains and, perhaps, in the mountainsides, and would be very difficult to find. But those were his only hope of being able to cross the Kalahari.

He could get some help from the map – the latitudes and longitudes of these water holes were marked in his military map. He had all the instruments – the sextant, the astronomical chart and other tables that Alvarez used to find out their exact location. But he had never learnt how to use them, and now there was nobody who could teach him. So, he would have to depend on his guardian angel who had brought him so far; surely, he would not fail him now? He would go across to as far to the north-east corner of the Kalahari as he could manage, and then he would commend his soul to his Gods and go across.

On the third day, he found the first water hole – a tiny crack in the boulders, filled with muddy water, so hot that it almost scalded his hands. Somehow, he managed to drink his fill and rested in the shade of the boulders for a while.

The desert grew more and more difficult for him to cross. In the next few days, all the remaining signs of animal and plant life vanished from the desert surface. Earlier, a few insects could be seen in the light of the campfire; now there were none.

The temperatures in the Kalahari were really extreme. Fiery hot during the day and freezing cold at night. Shankar's hands and legs would be frozen stiff at dawn, and he'd really want to light fires at night, but could not afford to as he was running short of firewood. Earlier, he could find dry twigs and branches strewn all about the desert plain, but now these too were becoming scarce.

A few days later, he ran out of water as well and had no idea where the next water hole was. Without being able to read the map and find out exactly where he was, finding water in this desert was worse than finding a needle in a haystack. But he had to find water, and he had to find it fast, otherwise he would have to face a slow and painful death. He had a long way to go before he reached safety, and he had come too far to turn back.

At dusk, he climbed a large dune to survey his surroundings. As far as the eye could see, it was all sand. Towards the east, the land seemed to climb to a range of hills. In the reddish light of the setting sun, he saw a small stone hill not very far from where he was, and there was also a small cave in the hill. Such hills of granite were quite plentiful throughout this land; these were called 'kopje' in Transvaal and Rhodesia. The kopje and the cave looked inviting to Shankar – they could provide some safety from the chill of the night.

That's where Shankar decided to set up his camp for the night.

Chapter 3

$\mathcal{H}$E MOVED ALL HIS MEAGRE BELONGINGS TO THE CAVE that very evening. He put in a pair of brand new batteries in his torch – he still had about a dozen pairs of batteries with him – and examined the cave in the torchlight. It was pleasant and cosy, like a nice little room. The floor was covered with lots of tiny pebbles. While examining the cave, he came upon something which caused him a lot of surprise. In one corner of the cave was a small wooden cask!

How did a wooden cask get here?

When he came closer to look, he got another shock. Leaning on the cave wall sat a skeleton with its bones bleached white and head turned towards the wall. It was wearing the torn remnants of what looked a woollen coat; its feet were shod with two heavy boots. Nearby, Shankar found an old rusted shotgun.

Next to the cask was a small bottle tapped with cork. Inside that was a roll of paper. Shankar uncorked the bottle and saw that it was covered with writing.

He went to look at the cask to see if it contained any water, and jumped back a couple of feet. An angry hissing sound and a large snake emerged from behind the cask with its head three feet above the ground. The snake hesitated for just one second before striking, and that one second was sufficient for Shankar. His Colt .45 shattered the head of the huge sand viper; the cask and the stone walls were spattered with bits of flesh and blood. Shankar thanked Alvarez for having trained him to be an absolute sure shot with the revolver and the rifle.

With a sense of deliverance, Shankar lifted the cask and found that there was still some water left in it. It smelt bad and looked totally black, but still it was water. Shankar lifted the cask and drank as much of that inkish black, foul-smelling liquid as he could. He poured the rest into his water bottles.

In the torchlight he examined the snake – nearly five feet in length and quite thick. He could survive on its flesh for quite a few weeks, if only he had some means of preserving it!

Shankar built a little fire from some wood he found in the cave. Now he felt he could relax and read the paper he had taken from the bottle. He took it out of his pocket, smoothed it out on his leg and started to read it in the light of the fire. To his pleasant surprise, the note was written in English.

Chapter 4

I AM CLOSE TO DEATH. I FEEL THAT TONIGHT WILL BE MY LAST night on earth. If, by any chance, some traveller comes to this cave while trying to cross this terrible desert, maybe he will find this paper and read about my last days.

Two days ago my donkey died in the desert. There was one cask of water left on its back. I have carried it into this cave. I am ridden with fever, I have not eaten for many days and I have no strength left in my body.

I am twenty-six years old and my name is Attilio Gatti. I was born in the famous Gatti family of Florence – I am a descendant of the great admiral Riolino Cavalcanti Gatti, who had fought and defeated the Turks at the Battle of Lepanto.

I studied with distinction at the Universities of Rome and Pisa. But my family is full of renowned travellers. The sea has enticed every generation of my family, and I was no exception.

While going to the Dutch East Indies, our ship foundered and sank near the western coast of Africa. Seven of us reached the shore somehow. I do not know what happened to my other shipmates. We somehow managed to make our way through the dense forests of the coast, and found refuge in a village of natives belonging to the Shefu tribe.

We heard about a huge diamond mine from the natives. The mine was deep in a very mountainous land, hidden in a dense and dangerous forest – that's all we could understand from their conversation.

We decided that we had to find the mine, come what may. My colleagues elected me their captain, and we set off on our quest. We pushed through impenetrable forests towards that totally unknown mountainous country. None of the villagers were willing to come with us as guide – they had never travelled to this country and did not know where it could be found; also they had heard that the forests around the diamond mine was guarded by a vicious evil spirit, who never allowed anyone to come back alive out of the forest.

We were determined to go ahead. We were all young and red-blooded and were not scared by the tales of evil spirits from illiterate African villagers. We pressed forward.

Two of our companions died in dire circumstances after suffering great hardships. My other four friends wanted to turn back. But I was not going to go back defeated. I am the scion of the great Gatti family; defeat is not in our blood. As long as I live, I know only one way to go – forward. I refused to turn back, and drove my companions deeper into the forests.

My body is now destroyed. The messenger of death will arrive tonight to take me on my journey into the next world. How beautiful is our little lake, Serino Lagrano, with our family palace, Castillo Riolini, on its bank! From here deep in the forests of Africa, I can smell the sweet flowers of our orange orchard next to our lake. I can hear the beautiful sound of the silver bell of the little church on the slopes of the hill behind our palace.

I am writing nonsense – the fever is getting stronger and I am losing my mind. I must force myself to write about what happened – I don't think I will last much longer, and I must not waste time.

We found those mountains; we went to those impenetrable forests.

We found that diamond mine. We found the river whose banks are strewn with diamonds. We found the source of the river – inside a huge and fearsome cave. I had entered that cave, and found hundreds of diamonds strewn all over the river bed, the river banks and the floor of the cave, like many small pebbles. The stones were clear, crystalline, tetrahedral in shape and yellow in tinge. The traders in the diamond markets of London and Amsterdam have never seen such diamonds!

I have also seen the demi-god, the evil spirit, the guardian of the forest, the mountain and the mine. I have seen it from afar, in the light of a flaming torch, made hazy by its smoke. It was a monstrous sight – I was saved from an attack by the flaming torch I held. Perhaps he lives in the same cave – I think that is why the natives speak of him as the protector of the mine.

It was time for us to return and that is where things began to go wrong. Accursed is the day on which I found the diamond mine! Accursed is the day on which I told my companions about the diamonds! When I took them back the same evening to the cave to show them the diamonds, I could not find a single stone. In the darkness of the cave that evening, with lighted torches in our hands, we searched for hours among the various streams that made up the river, but could not find a single stream in which we found a single diamond pebble. Not one solitary pebble.

My companions were simple, uneducated sailors. They thought I wanted to cheat them, that I wanted to keep all the diamonds and not share the wealth with them. I knew they were planning revenge, so I was alert and on the lookout for anything that could happen. Suddenly, the next evening, all four of them attacked me with knives. I was not really surprised; it was their turn to be surprised. They did not know who they were dealing with. I am Attilio Gatti. They did not know that in my veins runs the blood of ancestors like Riolino Cavalcanti Gatti, who had fought in the Battle of Lepanto and sent many barbarians to hell! I studied at the Santa Catalina Military Academy, where I defeated the best fencer in the district, Antonio Dreyfus, in a duel with knives.

My knife killed two of them. The other two were severely wounded and did not live to see the morning. But they had injured me in the fight, quite seriously. I could not stay in the cave. I had to escape the maze of the streams and somehow reach civilisation, if I wanted to save myself and my new-found riches.

I struck out in an easterly direction, hoping to reach the Dutch colonies. But now, I cannot go any further. They had knifed me in the lower abdomen; the injury has not got any better – in fact, the cut has turned poisonous. Along with the pain came fever. Why did they want to kill me? I did not want to cheat them or do them any harm. They were my friends, my companions; we had fought so many hardships together. The thought of cheating them, of depriving them of their share of riches had never crossed my mind. Oh, why did they want to hurt me!

I am the owner of the biggest diamond mine in the world; I have been through much hardship and imperilled my life to discover this, so it is mine. You, who are reading these words and understanding what I have written, you are doubtlessly an educated man and a Christian. Please, I have just one request of you – give me a burial befitting a devout Christian. For this favour to me, I am giving you the rights to the mine I have discovered. The treasures of the Queen of Sheba pale compared to the riches I have given you.

I am dying. I cannot fight death any longer. But what a terrible place is this desert where I must die! There is not a single sound – not even that of a cricket. The earth has such strange places! Throughout the day, I have been thinking that I will never again see the poplar-covered banks of our lake Serino Lagrano. I will never see the fourteenth century church on the banks of the lake; I will never again hear the sound of its silver bell; I will never again see my home, Castillo Riolini, looking like a Moorish palace sitting atop the hill; I will never again set my eyes on the green fields and vineyards of Umbria, through which flows the little river Dora.

I am delirious again. My end is nigh. I have dragged myself to the door of this cave so that I can see the countless stars in the sky when I finally pass from this world. Those inspiring words of St Franco are running through my mind:

> *Praised be my Lord*
> *For the gentle breeze*
> *For the tranquil air*
> *For the Mother Earth*
> *For the blue clouds*
> *For the sky above*
> *For the many stars*
> *For the good days and the bad days*
> *For the death of the body*

Oh! One more thing. Hidden in my boots are five large diamonds. I give these to you, my unknown friend, who is reading these words. Do not forget my last request. May the blessings of Mother Mary always be with you!

Commander Attilio Gatti
1880, possibly the month of March

Chapter 5

A LONG THIRTY YEARS HAD PASSED SINCE HIS DEATH AND, during this time nobody had entered this cave, nobody had perhaps even passed by this kopje. Finally, someone had discovered his body and learnt about his story.

Sad, unfortunate youth! Shankar felt a kinship, a brotherhood with the young man whose story was written on the piece of paper he held in his hands.

The cave that Gatti had described *must* be the same cave in which Shankar had got lost and almost died! He quickly removed the boots from the feet of the skeleton and sure enough, out dropped five pebbles! These were exactly like the ones he had seen in the cave which he had used as signposts during his wanderings; in fact, he still had one of them in his pocket! He brought it out – yes, all the six pebbles were absolutely alike! That proved it: he had discovered the same cave as Gatti. He had seen innumerable such pebbles on the shores of the various watercourses in the caves, and indeed in the beds of the streams.

Alvarez and he had sacrificed everything – Alvarez had even lost his life – to find this diamond mine; they had travelled long distances, been through untold sufferings, and spent nearly six months wandering aimlessly in the Richtersveldt mountains and forests. And, purely by chance, when he was trying to find a way to civilisation and safety, he had found it. How was he to know that, in this place, diamonds were lying in their hundreds, in fact in their thousands, as small pebbles, inviting whoever came to help themselves! If he had known that those were diamonds, he would have filled up all his pockets and bags with those innocent-looking pebbles!

He had found it by accident. *How will he ever find it again?* He had not made even a sketch map about its location; he had not left any signs near the caves. There was nothing that could help him find it again. And find it again he must. He planned to go back and find the mine but he had no idea how, since there was nothing to help him.

Shankar's thoughts went back to the last moments of Alvarez's life; he had said, 'Shankar, let's go! I can see a king's ransom hidden in the cave. You can't see it, but I can. Let's go!'

Shankar buried the skeleton in the cave. Breaking the cask, he made a rough cross from the rotten wood and the rusty nails which had held the cask together. He fixed the cross at the head of the grave of that brave young man. He prayed for the peace of his soul to all the Gods he worshipped.

He rested in the cave for the day and left its shelter the next day at dawn, taking the pebbles and the letter with him.

One thought kept haunting him. Nobody who had gone to find the accursed mine had ever returned. Attilio Gatti and his friends, Jim Carter, Diego Alvarez – all were gone. Who knew how many others had lost their lives in search of those mines? Was it now his turn? Would he have to leave his bones in this desert, to get bleached in the pitiless sun, perhaps to be discovered by some future traveller?

Part 13

Chapter 1

*S*HANKAR TOOK SHELTER BEHIND A HEAP OF BOULDERS. IT was midday and the desert was burning. His thermometer recorded the temperature as 135° Fahrenheit – much too hot for a human being to walk in. He was afraid of this desert, this killer of men. If he could somehow get across this terrible land, he was convinced that he would be able to reach some human settlement. He had been told that there were lions in the Kalahari Desert. He did not fear them. He had two rifles and about a dozen bullets. Why should he be scared of mere lions? What he was afraid of was the demon called thirst, from whom there was no deliverance.

He had heard about mirages. He had read about them in books before, but that day, he actually saw them. Once, it appeared far away in the north-east, and then, in the south-east – but both times they were almost identical. He could see a large mosque or a church, with a large dome, many palm trees surrounding it and, in front, a large, shimmering lake filled with water.

In the evening, he could spy the faint outlines of a mountain range far away among the low lying clouds on the horizon. Was he imagining things, he thought. There was only one large mountain in the east, a mountain large enough that could be seen from here, and that was the Chimanimani range at the border of southern

Rhodesia. So, was he coming to the end of the dreaded Kalahari Desert? Had he really succeeded in crossing it on foot?

He kept on walking deep into the night. At ten o'clock by his watch, he looked again at the horizon – yes, there it was! Clearly, in the bright moonlight, he could make out the line of the mountain range far away in the east. *Thank you, God! Thank you that it is real. After all, one cannot see mirages in the moonlight,* he thought.

Perhaps he was now getting towards safety! Maybe now he could look forward with hope of being saved! Perhaps he would be able to return to his darling mother, living in poverty in his beloved Bengal, and show her that her hardships were at an end, that he was indeed the owner of the largest diamond mine in the world, won by his own bravery, suffering and hard labour.

After two days of walking, he reached the foothills of the mountain range. He realised that he would have to cross the mountains, there was no other way of going to the other side. Either he crossed the mountains, or he went round them towards the south, which meant a walk of twenty-five miles in the desert. Twenty-five miles! He was not willing to take even one more step in the desert.

He would go across the mountains, he decided.

This was a momentous decision, and he nearly paid the ultimate price for this. He had underestimated the mountains in front of him. These were almost twelve to thirteen thousand feet high – crossing them was not an easy matter. Sure, he had crossed the Richtersveldt Mountains, which were even more difficult. But, he had forgotten that he had Alvarez to lead the way. Now, he was completely on his own.

Chapter 2

𝒯HE FORESTS IN THE CHIMANIMANI RANGE WERE NOT VERY dense, so Shankar could climb quite fast. He stopped for rest and to reconnoitre but could not find a way to get ahead from this point. He looked for the path he had used to climb up, but couldn't find it either! He somehow had the feeling that he had moved some thirty degrees south from the place he had begun to climb from the plains. He could not explain his instinctive feeling; neither could his instruments tell him why he felt he had gone astray.

He kept on going forward. But why did he get the feeling that he was taking too long to cross only some seven or eight miles? When he looked at the sun and tried to fix his position, he appeared to be going in the right direction at the right pace, but why did he still have the feeling that there was something wrong, something seriously wrong?

On the third day in the mountains, he faced another problem. The previous day he had stepped on a loose stone and hurt his knee. He had not paid much attention to his discomfort at that time, but now he could hardly put any weight on that foot. His knee had swollen to twice its normal size, and the pain was really severe. He would have to stay in the camp till his knee got better. There was no way he could climb up and down the mountains till then. He had to depend on the little food and water he had collected during his climb. But he would have to move around the camp to hunt and add to this little stock of food, just in case he was stuck here for a few days. Fortunately, the camp was on a flat ground, so he would not have to climb.

He could not take it anymore. He just wanted to lie down and sleep. Even if that was his last sleep, from which there was no awakening, so be it. Every step took so much effort. There was something wrong with his heart – after every few steps, he felt his heart racing, thumping against his rib cage; he had to stop and let his heartbeat slow down. His youth and health had been destroyed in these long months of severe hardship, lack of food, superhuman effort, and extreme deprivation. There was very little left of Shankar's physical strength.

On the fourth day, he leant back on a tree trunk. There was no more food left – the last scraps had been finished the previous evening. He had been carrying his rifles but in vain – he had not seen a single animal since noon, when he had stalked a deer. But he had left his rifle at the base of a tree some fifty yards away, and when he came back with it the deer had gone. Try as he might, he could not find it again. There was a little water left in the bottle, enough for a couple of mouthfuls, and he had to find a stream to refill it and soon, but his swollen knee made movement even more difficult, and the pain was now really unbearable.

He looked through the trees. In the clean, crystalline atmosphere he could see clearly for a very long distance. Far away ahead, he could see clouds covering the peaks of dark, blue-hued mountains. In the south-west, the Kalahari Desert covered all that the eye could see, all the way to the horizon. Down south were the Wahokuhok Mountains, and a long way behind that was the Paul Kruger mountain range, like a bunch of clouds floating just above the horizon. He could not see anything in the direction of Salisbury – a higher section of the Chimanimani range had blocked everything in that direction.

He also saw something that made him really afraid. The vultures that he had noticed in the afternoon were still circling up in the sky. He had thought that they had found a dead animal somewhere in the forest. But, maybe they were waiting for him? Did they sense that he was on his last legs and that they would not have to wait very long for a banquet?

Late in the evening, a slight noise made him fully alert. A grey wolf was looking at him from behind a large stone. In the darkness, the wolf was almost indistinguishable from the surroundings. In the light of the campfire, he could make out the edges of his ears, the long white fangs and the long red tongue and, of course, the eyes like burning coals. When Shankar looked at it, the wolf slunk back into the darkness.

Did the wolf also know something, like the vultures? Shankar had heard from African tribes and European travellers that animals have a sixth sense – they come to know of many things much before humans. Was his death one of those things?

It got very cold in the night. He had collected some dry branches and twigs before making his camp. The campfire could keep him warm for as long as it would burn and give him a little circle of light, inside which he could feel safe.

Some animal came and sat just outside the circle of light; he couldn't make out its shape immediately in the darkness. After a while, he recognised it as a coyote, an animal similar to a dog. Another coyote came, then a third... As the night progressed, more and more of their kindred joined them to form a group of more than a dozen. They sat all around him, around the fire, outside the circle of light which he had to keep burning, waiting with infinite patience.

What could they be waiting for? Shankar had to stay awake – he just could not afford to fall into a slumber. He shivered, not just from the cold. Those waiting coyotes were to him the harbinger of bad luck. Were they really waiting for his death? Would he be one more sacrifice to the gods of the diamond mines in the Richtersveldt?

He was so rich, rich beyond the dreams of avarice, as Shakespeare had written in one of his plays Shankar had read in his college days. Even if he could never come back to claim the diamond mine, the diamonds he was carrying were worth at least two or three lakh rupees. What could he not accomplish with that money! If he could only return to his village with that amount of money! He would be able to build his parents a nice, large house. He would be able to find grooms from good families for the poor girls in his village and give them good dowries. He would be able to make the last days of the poor and helpless old people in his village so much more comfortable and painless.

But, now it looked like none of these things would happen. That they would remain dreams, forever unfulfilled. Instead of wasting his time dreaming of the impossible, wouldn't it be better for him to face his approaching last days with courage? He would rather fill his eyes and his heart with the sight of the black sky lit up by countless bright stars, the black, silent, sombre beauty of the mountains and the desert, just like Attilio Gatti had done so many years ago. Shankar's destiny was tied up with Gatti and the others who had gone before: Jim Carter, Alvarez and countless others.

The night grew deeper and colder. Shankar remained awake to see if the coyotes had come closer. He picked up a piece of burning wood from the fire and threw it at the nearest group of coyotes – they withdrew for now. But they could afford to wait – slowly, silently, but surely they crept back towards the circle just outside the light of the fire. They knew that their prey was close at hand, and this prey would not be able to escape.

The wolf he had seen in the evening was also out there keeping vigil. Shankar had seen it a few times, sitting a little distance away from the circle of coyotes.

Shankar would have to stay awake. If he dozed off, maybe the coyotes and the wolf would tear him to pieces alive! From time to time, he picked up branches from the fire and threw them at his tormentors. But they never went away. In fact, he noticed that the coyotes and the wolf had been joined by a couple of hyenas as well.

He felt utterly helpless in such a dangerous situation. Here he was, alone, three-and-a-half-thousand feet up the side of the mountain, in an area completely devoid of human population. In front of him was a small fire; all around him was the total blackness of the African night. Overhead, the sky was lit by millions of stars like tiny faint electric bulbs; a little below him sat a bunch of coyotes, hyenas and a wolf, waiting to sink their hungry teeth into his flesh.

But this was the kind of death he would prefer. At least he was not dying slowly and painfully of malaria in his bed in the village; he was dying like a brave man, like a hero. All alone and on foot, he had crossed the deadly Kalahari Desert. Before he died, he would leave his name carved in stone somewhere in the Chimanimani Mountains. He would not be some unnameable unknown who died in the desert – after his death he would be famous as an explorer and traveller. He had discovered the huge diamond mine, all alone and without any help. After Alvarez's death, he had escaped from the maze of the mountains and the forests, again all on his own. And he had also come all this distance from the Richtersveldt Mountains and forest, all on his own.

Now, his time had come. He was sick and the injury hampered his movements. But he had not given up; he was still fighting. And he would fight till the very end. He was not afraid; he still had courage. He was not a coward; he was a brave man. Life and death was a game played by the fates; if he lost, that would not be his fault!

Chapter 3

*I*T WAS GETTING LIGHTER IN THE EAST. THE COYOTES, THE hyenas and the wolf vanished with day break. The day grew brighter and hotter – the merciless sun started to burn the ground and the stones around the camp. The band of vultures came back from somewhere, some settling on the ground, some on the branches of a few trees in the distance, and the rest circling overhead. They seemed to ask him: *Where will you escape? You have only a few more days to go, so do your best to enjoy this little time you are left with. We can wait; we are in no hurry.*

Shankar did not feel hungry and had no desire for food. But he had to eat in order to survive. He shot a vulture and roasted its flesh on fire. He had eaten vulture meat in the past but had never really relished its taste. Like it or not, this was now his only food. It was a strange tit-for-tat situation: he was eating their flesh today, maybe tomorrow they would eat his!

His shadow fell on a nearby stone. Suddenly, he thought he had been joined by another man. He started talking to his own shadow, before he realised his mistake. Maybe he was losing his mind! Maybe he was ill, or suffering from high fever. His thoughts were becoming all jumbled up. Alvarez... Attilio Gatti... mountains... dense forests... an unending sea of sand... Maybe the lack of sleep last night was taking its toll. Now it was getting darker. He must catch some sleep before night.

He fell into a troubled sleep.

What was that? A strange sound woke him up and he sat up hurriedly. Where did it come from? It did not sound like anything familiar to him in the forests or the mountains. He tried to fix the direction from which it was coming. The only thing he could make out was that it was coming closer.

He suddenly looked up. And there he saw it. Something large and shiny was going across the sky, high above his head. An aeroplane! He had read about these and even seen pictures in books, but this was the first time ever he had seen one.

He stood up and waved his shirt, waved a large branch, shouted and screamed at the top of his voice – all in vain. He could not attract the attention of the pilot. The plane kept on flying and disappeared far into the violet haze of the Paul Kruger Mountains.

Maybe another plane will fly the same way! What a strange creation this was, he thought. He had never seen an aeroplane in India, and he felt lucky that he had finally seen one.

He decided that he must make a large fire and a lot of smoke with leaves and branches, thinking that in case another plane went this way, the pilot would surely see the smoke and want to investigate.

Thankfully, the noise made by the aeroplane had scared off the vultures.

Nightfall brought back the coyotes, the hyenas and the wolf, and Shankar had to maintain the sleepless vigil once again. How could he keep himself safe from these creatures? A loud sound would certainly drive them away, but that would mean wasting a bullet. He had only a handful left. If he ran out of ammunition, he would certainly die of hunger. But he would have to drive them away. Deeper in the night, even more hyenas joined the gang. They had lost their fear of flaming branches.

Shankar dozed off for a moment. He suddenly woke up to find that the wolf had crept up really close to the camp. Another moment and the wolf would have charged at him. He picked up his rifle and shot at the beast but his weak hands couldn't keep the rifle steady, and the wolf escaped unhurt.

Early in the morning, Shankar found that the wolf had once again crept up very close. The coyotes were very patient; the wolf was looking for an opportunity for attack.

With the false dawn, all the animals vanished once more. Shankar sat next to the embers of the fire and fell asleep almost immediately.

He woke up with a start. Something, some loud sound, had woken him up. The sound was still ringing in his ears. Somebody had fired a gun! But how could that be? Who could possibly be brave or foolhardy enough to be travelling here?

He had just one more bullet left. Trusting his luck, Shankar loaded his rifle and fired: if death, here in the wild, was his fate, so be it!

In answer, he heard the sound of a gun firing twice.

In his joy and excitement, Shankar forgot that he had an injured ankle, that he could not drag himself very far. He had run out of bullets but he could still shout. He climbed painfully on top of a rock and started shouting at the top of his voice. He waved a branch he had brought with him while his eyes searched for more branches and twigs which he could start a fire with.

A survey team was on its way from Kimberley to Cape Town, to survey the Paul Kruger Mountains. On their journey, they had camped in the north-eastern corner of the Kalahari Desert, at the foothills of the Chimanimani Mountains. It was a large team, with seven half-track vehicles suitable for difficult terrain. In addition to African coolies and servants, there were nine Europeans in the team. Four of them had climbed up to the first range of hills in the mountains, searching for deer.

The sound of rifle in this uninhabited country surprised the survey team. They fired back and waited for a response. Not finding any, they started looking for the source of the sound. They finally found him. On top of a rock, on a higher range of hills, stood a skeletal, ghost-like figure, dressed in the last remains of European clothes, eyes burning with fever, set deep in their sockets, waving his hands and shouting something at the top of his cracked voice.

The team ran to Shankar. He tried to say something to them, which they could not understand. Carefully, they brought him down, picked up his belongings and brought him to their camp. Shankar remembered being fed and given something to drink and lying down on a proper camp bed, after which he did not remember anything at all.

His travails had taken their toll on his body. By nightfall, he had a raging high fever. In his unconscious state, he did not come to know when his saviours put him on one of their half-track vehicles, drove him to Salisbury, and took him to the hospital. Nearly one month was to pass before he was pronounced healthy by the doctors, and he could step out of the hospital onto the main roads of Salisbury.

Part 14

Chapter 1

*S*ALISBURY! TO SHANKAR, THIS WAS A CITY OF DREAMS. He had finally reached the place that Alvarez had spoken of, the city he had set out to reach from the forests of the Richtersveldt Mountains.

He was standing in the middle of a large, almost European city. Large houses, banks, hotels, shops, wide tarred roads with pavements, electric trams running on one side, rickshaws being pulled by Zulu Africans on another, newspaper hawkers shouting out the headlines of the papers – everything that happens in a large city. All this seemed so new to him, so unfamiliar, as if he had never seen such sights before.

He had reached civilisation, but he was completely penniless. He had no money, not even a few coins to buy himself a cup of tea. Nearby he saw a large shop selling soaps and perfumes, run by an Indian. The sight of a familiar face made him very happy. It had been such a long time since he had seen anyone from his homeland.

The shopkeeper was a Muslim gentleman, a Memon from western India. One look at Shankar and he realised that he was poor and had just recovered from serious illness. He gave Shankar two rupees and advised to visit an Indian businessman who could certainly help him.

Shankar gratefully took the money. He told the shopkeeper that he was accepting the money as a loan, and as soon as he could raise some money, he would come back to return it and the shopkeeper must not refuse. On the main road, he found an Indian restaurant. It was a temptation not to be resisted; it had been ages since he had tasted Indian food. He spent one of his two rupees eating his fill of *puris*, *halwa*, mutton cutlets, cake and other specialities of the restaurant, and followed it up with two cups of coffee.

On the table, he found a newspaper which was a few days old. One of the headlines riveted his attention. It read:

Amazing Experience of National Survey Team.

Discovery of an Indian in the Desert – Rescued from the Doors of Death.

The story of His Incredible Adventures.

Beneath these sensational headlines was Shankar's photograph, followed by a totally fictitious account of his travels, complete with imaginary quotes from him. He smiled – he had not told his story to anybody.

The paper was the *Salisbury Daily Chronicle*. He went to their office and introduced himself. This caused an immediate sensation. He was instantly surrounded by reporters and other staff. He learnt that the newspaper had been trying to find him for weeks. He told the story of his journey and rescue in the Chimanimani Mountains. They paid him fifty rupees, from which he repaid the loan he had taken from the Memon shopkeeper.

He also wrote an article about the volcano, which he called Mount Alvarez, and his miraculous escape from its violent eruption. The story of the discovery of an unknown volcano in Central Africa created quite a buzz. Some people believed it, while others were highly sceptical. But Shankar did not tell anybody about the diamond mine, lest hundreds of people would rush to find it and rob him of the fruits of his labour.

He went to a large bookshop and bought a big bunch of books and magazines. He had not read anything for such a long time! In the evening, he went to the cinema – another pleasure which he had been deprived of for years. At night, he went to a hotel and, lying on a proper bed under a whirring ceiling fan and the light of an electric bulb, he opened a book. But he could not concentrate. He stood at the window looking down at the Prince Albert Victor Street. He watched the trams go by, rickshaws weaving their way through the traffic, sometimes even a few cars zipping past. He heard the sound of cups tinkling in the Indian restaurant and the buzz of conversation from the street.

His mind went back to his last night in the mountains – campfire, coyotes and hyenas around him, behind them a couple of wolves with eyes shining in the light. Which was true? That night in the mountains, or this night in the city?

Very soon, Shankar became a famous man in Salisbury. The hotel lounge was always filled with reporters and photographers, jostling with each other to interview him, take his photographs, or ask him to write articles for their journals.

He informed the Italian Consul General about his discovery of the remains of Attilio Gatti. After searching through old papers in the Consulate office, they could trace some part of the history of the unfortunate young man. They found in their records that, in August of 1879, Attilio Gatti, a young man from a noble family in Italy, had indeed reached the shores of Portuguese West Africa after a shipwreck. There were no further records about him. Between 1890 and '95, his relatives had frequently importuned the Consulates in East, West and South Africa about his whereabouts. Many attempts had been made to find any traces of Gatti, and substantial rewards had also been announced for information leading to him. But all these efforts were in vain. Finally, in '95, his relatives gave up hope and no further attempts were made to find him or gather any information about him.

With the help of the benevolent shopkeeper, Shankar went to the famous jewellers, Rydall and Moresby, on Black Moon Street where he managed to sell four of his diamonds for thirty-two thousand and five hundred rupees. The other two stones were valued at a much higher price but he refused to sell them. He wanted to take them home and give to his mother.

Chapter 2

THE BLUE OCEAN WAS BEAUTIFUL.

Standing on the deck of the ship which was taking him to Bombay, he watched the palm trees on the shores of the port of Beira in Portuguese East Africa slowly vanish in the distance, and thought of his strange experiences in Africa.

This is what life really is all about, he told himself. This was the way he had always wanted to live. Age is a wrong measure of a man's life. He had lived in eighteen months what another would do in ten years. Today, he was no longer a traveller, a vagabond – he was the co-discoverer of an active volcano. He would make Mount Alvarez famous throughout the world.

But right now, he was impatient to see once again the shores of his motherland, his India. He could hardly wait for his journey across the Indian Ocean to come to an end. He was eagerly waiting for the Rajabai Clock Tower of Bombay to announce that he was soon about to set foot on his homeland. And shortly after that, he would reach the quiet, peaceful, green, little village in Bengal, where it would soon be spring. The Bauls would be singing their songs, the little winding paths in the village would be covered with flowers from the drumstick trees, the nightingale would sing in the Bakul tree beside his house, his dinghy would draw up at the landing ghat, and he would, at last, reach home.

Chapter 3

Goodbye, Diego Alvarez, my dear friend! I am on my way home, but the only person I can think of now is you. There is a rare breed of men who consider the open sky as the ceiling above their heads, for whom the whole of the earth is the road they have to walk. You belong to that breed. Bless me from your last resting place, from the depth of the forests you are buried in. Bless me that I can be like you, as brave and courageous, and as impervious to joy and pain as you.

Goodbye, friend Attilio Gatti! You must have been my friend over many lifetimes.

The two of you have taught me the true meaning of that ancient Chinese proverb: It is much better to be a shattered piece of jade lying on the floor rather than a tile in the corner of the roof.

For now, Shankar's motherland was calling him and he couldn't ignore her call. But, he would have to return to Africa. He would spend some time with his parents in his home, but he would go back. He would try to form a company in India, and he must go back to those dense and dangerous forests of the Richtersveldt Mountains. He must go back to that little mountain stream, that cave of diamonds. He must find them again.

Epilogue

While in Salisbury, he had visited the South Rhodesian Museum and met its curator – the famous zoologist, Dr Fitzgerald. Among other things, he had spoken about the Bunyip.

Some time after his return to India, he got the following letter from Dr Fitzgerald.

THE SOUTH RHODESIAN MUSEUM
Salisbury, Rhodesia, South Africa

January 12, 1911

Dear Mr Choudhuri

I am writing this letter to fulfil my promise to you to let you know what I thought about your report about a strange three-toed monster in the wilds of the Richtersveldt Mountains. On looking up my files I find other similar accounts by explorers who had been to the region before you, especially by Sir Robert McCulloch, the famous naturalist, whose report has not yet been published, owing to his sudden and untimely death last year. On thinking the matter over, I am inclined to believe that the monster you saw was nothing more than a species of anthropoid ape, closely related to the gorilla, but much bigger in size and more savage than the specimens found in the Ruwenzori and Virunga Mountains. This species is becoming rarer and rarer every day, and such numbers as do exist are not easily to be got at on account of their shyness and the habit of hiding themselves in the depths of the high altitude rain forests of the Richtersveldt. It is only the very fortunate traveller who gets glimpses of them, and I should think that in meeting them he runs risks proportionate to his good luck.

    Congratulating you on both your luck and pluck,
    I remain,

                                Yours sincerely,
                         (Sd.) J.G. FITZGERALD